NINETY-NINE FLIGHTS OF FANCY FROM AN INEBRIANT NINETY-NINE DRUNKEN DISPATCHES FROM A HOLY MAN THE ECSTATIC SOUL OF A DRUNK NINETY-NINE PRAYERS FOR THE DROWNING NINETY-NINE BOTTLES [BECAUSE ONE IS NEVER ENOUGH] NINETY-NINE WAYS TO BECOME A DRUNKEN SAINT NINETY-NINE PROOF DISTILLED SPIRIT NINETY-NINE ECSTATIC FRAGMENTS FROM AN INTOXICANT NINETY-NINE DRUNKS: KNOWN AND UNKNOWN NINETY-NINE ANECDOTES AND EPIGRAMS FROM THE HIGH-LIFE NINETY-NINE FLIGHTS OF FANCY FROM AN INEBRIANT NINETY-NINE DRUNKEN DISPATCHES FROM A HOLY MAN THE ECSTATIC SOUL OF A DRUNK NINETY-NINE PRAYERS FOR THE DROWNING NINETY-NINE BOTTLES [BECAUSE ONE IS NEVER ENOUGH] NINETY-NINE WAYS TO BECOME A DRUNKEN SAINT NINETY-NINE PROOF DISTILLED SPIRIT NINETY-NINE ECSTATIC FRAGMENTS FROM AN INTOXICANT NINETY-NINE DRUNKS: KNOWN AND UNKNOWN NINETY-NINE ANECDOTES AND EPIGRAMS FROM THE HIGH-LIFE NINETY-NINE FLIGHTS OF FANCY FROM AN INEBRIANT NINETY-NINE DRUNKEN DISPATCHES

OTHER BOOKS BY JOSEPH G. PETERSON

NOVELS

SHORT STORIES

NINETY-NINE BOTTLES

JOSEPH G. PETERSON

TORTOISE BOOKS

CHICAGO, IL

For my old friends and fellow bartenders at Jimmy's Woodlawn Tap, who were the right teachers at the right time, I dedicate this book with gratitude:

Bill, Vito, Matt, Jim (RIP) & Jimmy Wilson (RIP)

It matters, because everything we say

Of the past is description without place, a cast

Of the imagination made in sound

    —*Wallace Stevens*

It doesn't have a name, only an address—a number in tin hammered to the heavy black door. When regulars refer to it, they simply call it "The Bar." It is a nondescript storefront on an otherwise busy street. You couldn't look it up in the telephone book or, nowadays, search for it on the internet. In other words, if you don't know it's there, then you don't need to know about it.

It's a dimly lit place. A ceiling fan stirs the dust motes in the pink luminescence of late afternoon. A jukebox turned on low plays the old standards. There are stories told again and again. Pour me another. The bartender pours. Hit me again. The bartender hits again. The walls are dark, and it's unclear if they're stained wood or painted. A bolted TV hangs down from one corner of the room and it is turned on low. The bar-back mirror is crowded with bottles, old dictionaries, and the accumulated bric-a-brac of fifty years includes, improbably, an old harpoon. Above the cash register is a framed inscription that the bartender often repeats to customers who complain about the service:

ENTRANCE NOT FOR EVERYBODY

—NOT FOR EVERYBODY—

Ninety-Nine

DRUNKEN NARCISSUS

You stare into your drink, you lift your mug and take a gulp, you set your mug down and then you go back to studying your own mug in the bar-back mirror. Who am I, you ask yourself, and what essentially belongs to me? It's a circular solipsistic mode of thought, and after a while of staring into that mirror like gorgeous Narcissus you could swear your head is ringed with glowing daffodils and you say, I am me. This is who I am. All of this glorious splendid godforsaken and cursed thing and thingliness is me.

Ninety-Eight

ESSENTIAL SONGS

You are of the opinion that a jukebox is an essential ingredient to a great bar. And this is a great jukebox. On it, you will play in heavy rotation: Patsy Cline's "I Fall to Pieces," Billy Holiday's "Strange Fruit," "Devil and the Deep Blue Sea" by Louis Armstrong and Billie Holiday, Bobby Darin's "Mack the Knife," Fats Domino's "Blueberry Hill," Gene Ammons' "Angel Eyes" (with that devastating sax solo at the end), and your very favorite song of all time, "Flamingo" by Duke Ellington, sung with suave vocal styling by Herb Jeffries. You play this tune every time you step into the Bar. It puts you in mind of something expansive and wonderful, akin to chilled Tanqueray gin martinis with two briny olives sunk like eyeballs in the bottom of the glass.

There is also Guy Lombardo's song and its lyrics are not only pink but they speak to you where you want to live, where you want to be:

> *Enjoy yourself, it's later than you think*
> *Enjoy yourself while you're still in the pink...*

Ninety-Seven

THE COLOR PINK

The color pink...what does it mean to a committed drinker such as yourself, half in the bag? The rosy-fingered dawn comes to mind—which brings back seafaring memories that you never had, but experienced only by proxy through the eyes of Odysseus. And the idea of plugging beeswax in your ears and tying yourself to the mast while you sailed past the singing sirens enrobed in fluttering pink silk—hold me back! The beauty! And, of course you think of coral at the bottom of the sea—for isn't the bottom of the sea comprised of crystalline blue water, white fine-grain sea sand, pink coral for cut pendants hanging from her ear lobes, and floating tendrils of green seaweed like a girl's hair as she motions with her pink-painted fingernails: Come hither. You hold your beer bottle to your ear as if it is a conch shell. You run your finger along the smooth inner pink lip of the conch shell beer bottle and think, there's something to it, this idea of the world in all of its pink splendor beckoning while you, with eyes turned inward, go on drinking, ignoring as much as possible the clarion call to go forth, join the world, prosper. No, you'd rather not. You'd rather stay in this sinkhole caught in some astral dream of pink splendidness, forgetting it all. Pour me a drink please, and leave me the fuck alone.

Ninety-Six

HARPOONIST AT THE BAR

Other things about the Bar that you like: it's stumbling distance from Lake Michigan and so it—to you, appropriately—incorporates sea motifs. There is a wood-spoked wheel for turning a ship, there are the old lantern-lamps with the blurred heavy glass domes that were formerly used to light a ship's cabin. There are anchor motifs behind the bar, and anchor hooks upon which you can hang your coat (preferably a yellow oil slicker), but most appropriately, it has an authentic whaler's harpoon with a hemp rope neatly coiled around its stem and a flanged barb at the business end ready to sink itself remorselessly and fixedly into whale blubber. You stare at that harpoon whilst you sit at the bar drinking hot toddies to fend off the cold, and you let your imagination travel where it might. What if, for instance, there was a whale swimming right now in Lake Michigan, a whale that has come down from the Saint Lawrence Seaway? What if there was some as-yet-undiscovered loathsome leviathan (akin to the Loch Ness monster) lurking in the murky bowels of our very own Lake Michigan? Why then, with this harpoon you just might stand on the high rocks of Promontory Point and hunt it.

There you stand, squinting out into dark lake. And there you see a whale fin stirring the water in the middle distance. You drop your arm back like a quarterback aiming for the end zone and you hurl the spiky thing at the monster and strike at its heart. And then hand over hand you bring him to shore and you gut him, cutting through the whale lard, and you study his innards like a clairvoyant looking for signs. But signs for what? And then it hits you: signs for the highlife.

Ninety-Five

BACCHUS IN THE STREET

You were packed into the bar—you and seemingly hundreds of people from the neighborhood—to watch your team win the championship victory. The fist-pumping, chest-pounding joy of that moment seemed to burst the bar like a ripened pod and you and all the others spilled like seeds into the streets singing and dancing and drinking and a Chicago paddy wagon showed up to impose order, but the cops just watched as you and the revelers had your party. This is what we were put on earth for—this right here, jumping up and down on the street singing and cheering with strangers. *Na Na Nana...Na Na Nana...Hey Hey Hey...Goodbye!*

In the days after, you would call your friend or he would call you and you would say: Do you have Bar-itis? That was a disease you got if you hadn't been to the Bar in a while. Yup, you would say or he would say, and you would recommend the local cure, a visit to the Bar. You carried on this tradition for several years until he moved away to Connecticut to start up his own business.

The night before he left you had one final round at the Bar. You untwisted one of the anchor hooks from the coat rack and you presented it to him. Here you go, buddy, you said. Carry this with you wherever you travel. Don't ever forget where you come from. You had a hug, then you stumbled out of the place.

It was the last time you ever drank with him.

Months later you learned he lost the anchor hook that night on the way home to his apartment. I was so drunk, he said.

Now you haven't talked to him in years. He went his way, you went yours, blown apart by the Trade Winds.

Ninety-Four

ALL THE TIME IN THE WORLD

You are just starting out and though you are just starting out you believe yourself to have been in this game a long time. You show up and you speak in a vernacular that doesn't quite synch with the place, but all the old-timers get the general idea. You sit next to one old-timer and when he gives you the cold shoulder you move on to another and when he looks at you like you don't know what you're talking about you go and find another regular at a different spot at the bar. You show up at unusual times—you have no predictable pattern, except that once you show up you drink until you can stand it no more and until you can no longer stand. You are too young to be marked by tragedy or pain—and yet your mother died and they don't know this and another thing they don't know is that your mother was a fucking bitch that you loved more than words can say so when she died you didn't know what the appropriate response was: whether to scream from pain or to scream from anger. When you sit down next to one old-timer he asks you what you're doing here and you tell him: drinking beer. When he asks why you would waste your time in a shithole like this, especially when the sun is shining and the world beckons, you tell him: I'm here for no reason at all and, frankly, what does it matter? I still have all the time in the world.

Ninety-Three

A SIMPLE THIRST

When you think about it, going back in time, your expenses were simple. You were just starting out. You cooked all your own food. You weren't a fancy cook. You cooked pork chops in butter with rosemary that you rubbed between your palms and garlic that you smashed with the flat end of a knife then you'd gather it up so your fingers smelled of it. You roasted chicken with salt and pepper and lemon, like the Greeks, and you fried eggs so perfectly that you considered yourself a master chef, and you drank Carlo Rossi wine out of a jug that you kept chilled in the fridge and you had a thirty-pack of Busch beer on hand which you purchased not because you liked the beer but because it was cheap and you liked to look at the picture of the mountains on the can while you drank. You kept cranberry juice in the fridge to mix with vodka that you stored on ice in the freezer and late at night, after returning from the Bar and not even remembering how you made it home, you would lie awake in bed wondering how to cure this unbearable thirst.

Ninety-Two

HOW TO RECOVER THE PAST

The past is closed. You only recover it with words. You sit there staring at the bar-back mirror trying to form the words that will tell you the story of your past. You practice the words every night trying to get them exactly right.

This is what you say to the man next to you and he looks at you trying to understand. We move through time, you say, and the prow of our ship is always cutting the water and the wake disappears behind it. But the saying seems so inadequate to the feeling of loss in your heart that you repeat yourself on and on through the night. You can see it so clearly: how the ship is always moving and how time is split by the prow of the ship and then you look behind at the receding wake and you feel such loss watching it disappear. Don't you understand what I'm saying? you ask the man. Your lips move. His eyes stare at you and in the noise of the bar not a sound is heard.

Ninety-One

PIPE DREAMS

What was the water like when the sun hit the wake of your ship turning the white froth of foam the color of the rosy-fingered dawn? Maybe you were sailing off the coast of Mexico and the screws of the ship were churning up the water in white jets, but already this ship you were sailing on was becoming a memory. As were the white birds that plummeted from the sky into the ship's wake, as was the smell of land coming off the island. A lady in a hat was on deck drinking a cocktail and reading a book. It was the prettiest thing you've ever seen: that lady in a hat sipping her cocktail and reading like she had all the time in the world.

You sit at the Bar sipping your cocktail and you try to read what will happen next. What can possibly happen next at a place like this?

Back then you wanted to be a writer. You were writing down anything that came into your head. You were trying to figure out how to write a story. How do you write a story? How do you write it so that when the reader sets the story down the reader feels both truth and beauty? Not just any truth, but the gasping truth that this is it exactly: this is what the world really is like— white birds plummeting from the sky, the smell of land from the distant island, the lady in a hat caught up in the sparkle and spray of the sea, and that warmth and glow, remembering the beauty of it all.

Ninety

DAYS OF WINE AND ROSES

She was drunk when you met her and you were drunk too and you went back to her place and both of you were stinking drunk and you lay on the couch and opened a bottle of wine and when you finished the bottle of wine you brought a six-pack of beer out of the fridge and started drinking that and when you were done with the six-pack you opened up a fifth of Jim Beam and you lay on the couch drinking Jim Beam until you passed out.

In the morning you woke up hung over and the sun was coming through the windows and it was more than you could bear but you wanted to stay drunk so the two of you headed over to the Bar and you had Bloody Marys for breakfast and at lunch you were drinking beer again and through the day you thought it would be fun to try some tequila because tequila put you in mind of Mexico even though you had never been there. And you cursed because the tequila bottle didn't have a worm in it. Doesn't tequila come with a worm? you asked. So you bought a bottle of mescal next and the two of you drank through the night in search of the worm with hallucinogenic properties and when you finally came to it you each put an end of the worm in your mouths and you pulled until it broke then she stuck her tongue in your mouth and for a while you didn't know whether you'd become the worm or whether the worm became you. And after that you didn't care.

Eighty-Nine

THE DRUNKEN BOXER

One day at the bar you sat next to a man who worked the back room of a grocery store collecting all the cardboard boxes that deliveries came in. There were the wax-coated cardboard boxes that the produce was shipped in, he explained, and there were also the regular cardboard boxes that nearly everything else came in. His job was to collect the boxes, and to put them in a baler. He'd press a green button: the baler would compact the boxes, then he'd wrap steel straps around the bales that he then cinched with a metal crimping tool. He'd lean into the bale with his shoulder to move it out and then, getting on a forklift, he'd scoop the bale up and put it on a stack of other cardboard bales behind the store. He couldn't have been older than thirty and when you asked him what's it like doing that kind of work every day? he took a sip from his vodka and sighed, Oh. Aches and pains and my boss is an asshole who treats me like an animal. If it weren't for him I'd be happy there. If it weren't for him and these aches and pains. You do this kind of work day after day and your body never stops hurting. But when you're young you can do anything.

You smile at him like he's right, because he is. When you were young, anything was possible. That's when you drank like a monster and never once looked over your shoulder.

Eighty-Eight

YOUR GIRL

She slaps you. You slap her back. When she asks why you slapped her you say: Because you slapped me. Her slap was unasked for and unexpected—in that way it was almost designed to make you laugh like a joke. What's more there was something in her eye—something that was endearing. But you didn't laugh. You were on your fourth beer. There was nothing funny about getting slapped with all these people around, and what's more it set a bad precedent. And that's what you wanted to tell her but she was already out the door. You wanted to tell her she left you no other choice. Later, you refused to tell her even after she apologized that there were countless choices you might have made that night, and foremost among them, you might have laughed. You see now that that would have been quite a decent thing to say. You might have laughed after she slapped you but you didn't.

Almost two years to the day she slaps you again. This time because you broke her heart. You don't do anything for a moment and in a moment she's gone. That's when you walk to the fridge and open another beer.

Eighty-Seven

THE VOYEUR

You stand behind the building with the bartender and he smokes a cigarette and tells you how he peers into people's bedrooms with binoculars. He was always on the lookout for some unsuspecting female standing naked in her room. And you remember him saying he knew of one woman. She was always getting naked and she was hot. Hot. Those were his words. You were fascinated by that—that he would tell you such a thing. That he would talk about peering into other bedrooms as if you weren't standing there listening to him.

Later while he was serving you a drink at the Bar you two locked eyes. He stared right into your eyes as if he were looking through those binoculars into the illuminated and solitary rooms of your soul. You blink to close the shutters, but it's too late. He'd already seen all he needed to see.

Eighty-Six

THE DRUNKEN SOVERIGN AND HIS REALM

There you sit. The afternoon light is slanting through the window casting shadows among the dust motes. The day is caught in a lull between the afternoon rush and happy hour. It's not a long lull, but suddenly you alone possess it. There's one bartender down at the corner of the bar staring at the TV and a short-order cook is clanging away at some pots in the kitchen. How did it come to pass that without even thinking about it or planning it, you have become sole monarch of this emporium? You look around at the empty barstools and you think, this is my kingdom, at least for this moment, and this moment is mine too. Suddenly everything in your life that has been so inexpressible wells up inexpressibly in you and you want to put the precise word to it—you want to name that tumult of feeling in one striking phrase of perfect statement. Something beautiful as peacock feathers or a flower arrangement. Then it hits you. This is who I am, you think. I am this glorious kingdom. I am the pink light illuminating the dusky corners of this divine and disorderly place. I am a drunken god wrapped in robes of holy fire. Then you stare at yourself in the bar-back mirror and smile at the company you keep.

Eighty-Five

SACRED BULL

A tall man in a hat walks into a bar.

This is not a joke. You are sitting there one afternoon drinking shots of tequila. There is only you and the bartender and a cook clanging away at some pots and pans. What is the cook doing in there? What is the bartender doing? Who are you and why are you sitting here in the desultory lull of the afternoon? And you might answer: I am sitting here because I believe in honoring the moment that is given me. You might answer: I am here because I refuse to be one of those who toil ceaselessly on the rack to get ahead. You might answer: I am here because I am looking to become a sacred bull, one with the sacred flow of time and oblivious to, but ever waiting for, the final shock that will come like a heaved cutlass blow to my neck.

You might only say, on the other hand, that I am here because I have nowhere else to go or that I am a drunk, helplessly enslaved by the charms of tequila or that I am here only to see who next will come through the doors into this dank and despicable place.

That's when the tall man in a hat steps into the bar and just behind him the old regular whom you privately refer to as Blind-eyed Bob even though that's not his name. All the years you've both been coming here you've never exchanged so much as a hello. By the time he hangs his coat and takes his seat at the far corner of the bar it's precisely 4:00pm. This is his time now, Blind-eyed Bob's moment, and you've learned to cede your moment to his and to set your watch to it. Hello Blind-eyed Bob, you think. Hello tall man in a hat! Welcome. You sit there and drink, eyeing them, wondering...will they even notice you?

Eighty-Four

THE GRIM REAPER HEAVES HIS CUTLASS

Three hours later you turned your head to see Blind-eyed Bob, but he was gone. A moment later you heard him hit the floor with a bang. It was surreal. You were sitting at one corner of the bar; he was sitting at the other. You turned your eyes away for a moment to take in the late evening light filtering into the dark spaces of the bar and that's when it happened.

Blind-eyed Bob was half-blind and wore these thick glasses. He was an old man: large as a linebacker, but weight and age had slowed him down. What was his real name? Who was he? Where did he live? Who were his associates? Did he have any stories to tell? He might have once been a cop...or maybe a teacher? Or a truck driver? Or a linebacker. What were his stories? Why should you know what he did or who he was? He was just another soul drinking at the bar. You did know this: he showed up every night at exactly 4:00pm and he never missed a day. You could set your watch to him walking through the door. He'd walk to the end of the bar opposite you. He'd sit, order a rum and Coke, and nurse it for an hour or so, then he'd order another and then another. He was a solitary drinker. He was a solitary man. He fell off the back of his stool when you weren't looking and hit the ground with a bang.

In the commotion of the fall, there was the tall man with the hat. He took one look at you. He took one look at the body lying motionless on the floor, and without saying a word he slipped out the bar.

Then the ambulances came and four men with blue plastic gloves on their hands heaved and then hauled Blind-eyed Bob out on a gurney. Then the bartender brought the bar back under control, resetting the stool, cleaning the mess of beer bottles and ashtrays. When he was done, he went back to pouring beers, and you ordered one.

The next day there was the announcement that Blind-eyed Bob had died of a brain hemorrhage. A round of drinks on the house was ordered and there was a toast hoisted in his honor at exactly the moment—4:00pm— he would have walked through the door. It was, to say the least, an exciting time. Then everything went back to normal except no one ever sat in Blind-eyed Bob's seat. They kept it empty, waiting for him. You sit in your seat at your appointed hour and at 4:00pm every day you look to see if he's coming back. Blind-eyed Bob is gone. When you look in the corner where he sat, all you see is his ghost.

Eighty-Three

MERMAID

In your imagination you are in love with a bartender of unapproachable beauty—raven hair, dark skin, and unbelievable shapeliness—and what's more, she's younger than you by a decade. What was she doing at a place like this? It was a rotten place yet she was such a sparkling light. She frequently wore a low-cut aquamarine sequined dress. She moved about the place like a mermaid who'd just found her legs. In tight spots she squeezed past the other bartenders and she was all sensuality. It was all the physical contact you needed to see and it turned the otherwise prosaic and frantic moments of drinking into poetry—the likes of which you never again experienced until she was supplanted by another bartender, a prettier bartender by the name of Heather.

Eighty-Two

A TIGHT TIGHTROPE WALKER

You sit there at the table in the corner of the bar with a pitcher of beer all to yourself trying to erase once and for all the long-ago blow he gave you and the subsequent lifelong hurt whose name shall go unspoken. If you allow yourself to dwell on either the blow or the lifelong hurt, your mind, you have found, will get caught in a circular loop and once caught in this *buzzing feedback* there is no other choice but blackout drunkenness to turn it off and so you sit there like a drunken idol—unwilling to flinch or move lest too quick a gesture tear the wound open and push the mind where it dare not go.

Today, you have been fairly successful staying away from that awful place of hurt. As if on a tightrope, you move very carefully with incredible daintiness as you lift the beer mug to your lips and you think to yourself: I am a rock of unmovable stability married to the fluid gesture of a ballerina. You comprehend how crossing from this moment to the next without disturbing thought takes an act of supreme balance. Step. Pause. Step. You set the beer down. With all the effort that took, you look ahead and wonder how many steps to go.

Eighty-One

A HEAD OF CABBAGE

You have a cabbage in your refrigerator and it's been there for several weeks. You worry about it. You know it sleeps in the dark and sleeping in the dark causes spoilage. When you come home from the Bar you open your refrigerator and there it is caught in the refrigerator's cold light. It's pale green with thick white veins and ridges that somehow remind you of what? You cannot say, but all of a sudden you are a boy leaping in the creek and there up ahead pushing through the over-green vegetation is your barelegged mother. Mom...Mom...

In your mind you shut the door on the fridge and you take another sip of beer. At some point, you think, I will either have to eat the cabbage or I will have to throw it out. And it crosses your mind that you have no idea how to prepare such a thing as a cabbage. Certainly you don't know how to prepare something that reminds you of your mother's bare legs running barefoot through a creek while you followed, barefoot, shouting her name.

Eighty

NUMBERS MAN

Who am I? Let's apply the number six. That's the answer to the question, you think, somewhat victoriously. I am a six. While you sit drinking vodka you have no idea why the number six answers all the questions that are improbably welling up in your soul. You only know that when all of these questions well up at once, saying, quite simply: I am a six—seems to quell the clamor. I am a six you say again. I am a man, and I am a six. What that means suddenly is quite clear and also heartbreakingly profound: I am neither a seven nor a five. It's true, you think. No matter that the noise and racket of the bar and its crowds tonight are almost more than you can handle. No matter that you're half done in on vodka trying to keep things straight in your mind. You are a numerical iteration no different than all these other numerical iterations. It is true, that to know who you are is so very important if only because it brings clarity to the question of who you are not. In my case: I am neither a five nor a seven. That is because I am a six.

Seventy-Nine

THE WAGES OF ABSENTEEISM

This morning is Bloody Mary Day and perhaps that's what got you thinking. Or perhaps it was last night's dream whose vapors are still circulating through your emotional system.

You were sitting on the sun-warmed steps of the St. Thomas Church. The church was caught in the pink light of the dying day when she told you that she was leaving. An angel seemingly made from the greenest leaves of the old oak tree was drifting on the evening breeze headed who knows where? Where are you going? you asked.

I'm leaving.

What does that mean?

It means, quite simply, that I'm leaving. I want out and I'm getting out.

Then she says: You've been an absentee father. You're unreliable. I can never count on you for anything. You spend all of our money on drink. I have tried to reason with you but you can't listen to me. I'm taking the kids to my mother's house. They'll be better there.

And that was, as far as you can tell, the beginning of the end, though it probably ended much earlier than that.

What were you two doing on the steps of the old church? What was that green angel of leaves you saw flying overhead, and what did it portend? You fall into argument with yourself: I was sitting on the steps of a church, for Christ-sake! I've never been on the steps of a church before in my life and as far as I can remember, she wasn't Catholic or religious either. So why the steps of the church? Why that fucking green angel? Why?

That's when you remember to sip your Bloody Mary and repeat: I am a six.

Seventy-Eight

WRITER'S BLOCK GIVES WAY

You're in a capital mood today. If someone asked how you would describe yourself, you'd say, I'm in a capital mood. It's an old expression long out of use, but you don't mind sounding as if you're half-lost in antiquity. You sidle up to the bar and snap your finger and order a beer. This is how you like your beer: you like it from the tap directly into a Tom Collins glass and set on a coaster. You call the extravagant concoction 'A Golden Cadillac.' The bartender loves you and forgives your snap and humors you as you speak in lost and forgotten clichés. When he asks you what's the cause for your jubilant mood, you tell him that your writer's block has been conquered and in a snap you wrote a piece. A piece? he says, curious. Tell me about it. So you pull the piece from your pocket and read it to him verbatim. And as you read you slowly lick your thumb and turn the pages of your document.

When you're done reading you lift your eyes. They are luminous as if fired by the candles of the gods. You haven't felt so splendid in years. It reminds you of a weekend you had eating lobster in Cape Cod. You cracked the hard shells of tail and claw ravenous to get at the soft meat.

I've finally cracked the shell, you tell the bartender, and I've gotten into the soft meat of the matter and I'm dipping it in butter. Do you understand what this means to me?

I'm sure it means a lot, the bartender says. It has to, doesn't it?

Seventy-Seven

LONG-REMEMBERED SONGS

You found your mescal and by the end of the night you are perfectly happy. You stumble home through the streets looking into the apartment windows for signs of life. In your mind you are wrapped in an island air and you ride through the land of the dead on a unicorn horse carrying a bouquet of roses. That's when you start to chant at the top of your lungs the most beautiful words you know:

Forsooth, I have felt the bitter winds blow against my cheeks and have marched a fortnight across red-hot sands to the gates of Eldorado and I have seen its men with their women in silks and I have seen naked children at their hips and they stood in the shadows of doorways singing long-remembered songs of the sea...

Seventy-Six

THE SAINT PAULI GIRL ON THE BEER ADVERTISEMENT POSTER

You sip your beer, lift your head and stare at the Saint Pauli girl in the beer advertisement poster taped to the wall. You can't decide what it is about her but you establish an instant intimacy. Staring at you from the poster, she smiles just so, as in: Just so's you know, this is between you and me. Her eyes, not batting a lash, stare unblinkingly waiting to see if you'll concur, and you do. You have another sip of beer and now, you're friends.

She gazes into your eyes and sees down into the garbage chute that is your soul. It's a trash heap down there and you're filled with shame, but her eyes say: Trust me, I understand. And you do trust her. That she has the courage to do this moves you. That she is also pretty while she does this is inexplicable. That she's the Saint Pauli girl on the beer advertisement poster is beside the point.

She sees how you're all bound up and naked and twisted. So she unloosens, just a little, the knots that bind your hands and mouth. You take another sip of beer and say, thank you.

She gets all of your failings, your failures, your hurts. She sees your life has been a shitstorm. She sees the expiration date on who you might have become has gone past due, but she does not judge.

I know I'm an asshole, you tell her. I know my better days are behind me. I know.

As you pour your heart out to her, she listens and does not blink.

I'm evasive, you explain. I can't be counted on in a crisis. I've never learned how to tell the truth when it really counts. I've fucked over those who have only done me a good turn. I'm a bad seed. A rotten egg. I am lost and filled with pain.

Hush, her eyes say. Hush.

You commit a whole afternoon to looking at her; you have nothing else to do. She speaks to you in truth. Her eyes are pretty blue, and beneath the cream gauze of her blouse you see she's naked. See, her eyes explain, I can hold my nakedness close to you. You may look through the gauze of my blouse and see what you see. It's all there for you.

You smile at her and tip your drink, full of gratitude for having spent your afternoon with the Saint Pauli Girl.

Seventy-Five

A LEGEND RAISES HIS HAND THROUGH THE WATER

You try to remember your father tonight, which is odd.

Prior to tonight you had spent most of your waking hours trying to forget him. It was hard to do because even in death he seemed to force himself on you. But first the bartender asked you about your old man. And instead of getting upset you merely smiled and tried to humor him; after all, the bartender was your friend. And you explain to him about your dad, Yes, he had a yacht, you told him. Yes, he was famous in a way. Yes, he was a larger-than-life character and then his boat sunk in a gale and he died. Only this is not what really happened, but you can't bring yourself to say this any other way, so you shut up. When you tried to suggest to the bartender that you had nothing more to say about your dad, the bartender kept pressing. He asked: No, please tell me. Where did he harbor his yacht? I heard he had these parties...they're legendary...people come in here all the time talking of him.

And you say in the friendliest way possible: Give me another beer, please.

When he's pouring your beer, you try to look on the bright side. I was related to the man, after all. I am his blood. If he was legendary doesn't a little of that wash off on me? But in fact, it never has and that's what causes concern. You were small and went unnoticed.

When the bartender sets your beer down he steps away shaking his head in disbelief: My, oh my, your old man must have been something else!

You sit alone now and watch yourself in the bar-back mirror and barely moving your lips you quote from memory a few lines of the poem you wrote of the old guy to eulogize him. His funeral had been packed with hundreds of friends and luminaries; the vaulted space of the church held their resonance. It was the largest crowd you ever addressed. When you stood up to the lectern, you read—or rather shouted—as if you meant it:

> *Give me my father back and backwards*
> *He fell off the boat when I pulled him out*
> *He was drunk and dead his wrists slit*
> *I see him sinking now in the gloomy depths*
> *One hand reaching through the water,*
> *   screaming, son,*
> *And then he was sunk until I pulled him out*
> *But I saw that look in his eyes*
> *It regretted all that it let go.*
> *And then, when he saw me, it let go.*

Seventy-Four

DRUNKEN ROMANTIC HEAVES OATHES UPON THE PRESENT

Occasionally the rage roils up in you and before you know it you're screaming about the goddamned stupidity of it. The stupidity of the way the country is run, of the music the kids listen to, the stupidity of television, the stupidity of the talking heads, of politicians. You scream about the stupidity of the modern athletes all doped up on steroids and the stupidity of all the bosses you ever had. You rage against the stupidity of a world that has fallen far from grace and is doomed and ruined beyond recognition. You hate all the stupid rich idiots and the dumb political bastards that got away with it and you laugh at the rest of the jerks who got what was coming to them. Late into the night several beers and brandies in, you start mumbling about the venal, outlandish stupidity of all the women you have ever known and the stupidity of friends who have long since abandoned you and finally you launch into the venal stupidity of your own children. And you use that word to great effect, 'venal.' The venal stupidity! The bastard kids are just like their mother, the spiteful ingrates, and the world has gone to hell.

Of course, it wasn't always like this. And here's why—you take another sip of alcoholic elixir, you think it out very carefully and this is when you remember running down a beach of sand on a deserted coastal island that was white, the same virgin whiteness as a new-fallen snow, and it was as if the world were new and full of possibility.

You continue, Hell, I remember snow itself—that's right!—the way it used to fall in the days when there used to be whiteout blizzards before there was all this global warming; I remember when women were women and when they had manners and notions of respect and self-restraint and when men used to be quiet yet strong. That was when being a man was more prized than being a boy, but things change.

You grow quiet and just before blacking out you remember this bygone thing: the dried rice flung at your white bride on a spring day as she lifted her veil in the pink light and leaning toward you—her face radiant and soft—said, Please, kiss me. Kiss me!

Seventy-Three

The Puerto Rican butcher sips his rum and Coke. You talk with him about the old guy with the cane, Blind-eyed Bob, who tumbled dead off his stool. Who was he? Was he a teacher or something? A linebacker? Did you know him?

The Puerto Rican butcher tells you that the man who fell off his stool and died had been a machinist his whole life. He had a wife and two grown daughters. Then he tells you that the old man, whose actual name was Johnny Bright, had been the bombardier on a B-17 during WWII. He tells you that Johnny Bright had flown thirty-five missions over France and deep into Germany to blow up the ball-bearing plants. On D-Day Johnny Bright flew two missions over the Beaches of Normandy and he had once described the parachutes of the soldiers who dropped behind the lines in the early dawn hours of the invasion as glorious white flowers. Glorious white flowers, the butcher repeats. He tells you that Johnny Bright had to jump down into the hatch to kick a bomb loose that had failed to release. He lowered himself into the hatch. He held onto a thin metal bar and he kicked hoping that the bomb wouldn't blow. Another guy was operating the bomb bay, trying to make it open again. Meanwhile, the bar Johnny Bright was hanging from started to bend. Finally, the doors opened and the bomb let go. Bright watched it falling miles from its original target where it blew up in the town below. After the

Puerto Rican told that story, he pointed out the stupidity of Germany trying to invade France. Why would one sovereign nation take over another? What was Hitler thinking?

What about Stalin, you say. What was he thinking? What about Franco and Mussolini? What were they thinking?

They were sycophants, the Puerto Rican says.

Yes, you say. Murderous sycophants.

Aren't all sycophants murderous, he asks.

You sip your beer followed by a quick tequila shot then nod.

Then the Puerto Rican took a sip of his rum and Coke and smiled thoughtfully and said that Bright survived long enough to meet his end here. This is where he *chose* to die. Of all the places to die after what he saw—those parachutes falling behind German lines in Normandy like glorious white flowers—and he waited so many years later to die here falling off his stool like a potato.

Seventy-Two

BLOW MAN BLOW

You made it here drinking through the night to closing time. You have had too many beers and the tequila shots are messing with you. When the lights turn on and the bartenders call for last drinks, the ghost of Johnny Bright who is large as a linebacker and who has been staring at you for the past several hours finally gets up and walks over to you.

He offers you one more round.

He tries to engage you in conversation, which is odd because in life you and he pretended as if the other never existed. What is he trying to say to you? You try asking him but your words come out in a drunken mumble. He tries telling you but you can't hear him. It occurs to you that language is broken—there are too many gaps of meaning between words. If the gaps could only be repaired then the tattered cape of language could be flung like a mighty flag from the masthead, semaphoring all that you think and feel to the distant galleons. It's even more problematic, you realize, because there are seemingly irreconcilable differences between you and this ghost, and language seems non-transferable between the two unlike properties of your corporality and his phantasm—that's when he leans in close as if he has something urgent to tell you. And broaching the usual intimate spaces that naturally separate two civilized adults he clasps his hands behind your head and he puts his lips on yours and he blows into you as if you were a great trumpet. Lip to lip, you feel the surging wind of him strain the distant parts of your being as he says:

> *Behold, I am Johnny Bright the man you never said a word to. I fell off my stool like a potato but they, those young D-Day soldiers, they fell behind enemy lines like glorious white flowers.*

Seventy-One

VARGAS

He works as a night janitor in a bank in the Loop, and he has access to things. You have no idea what I have access to, he says. The art alone is unbelievable. It should be in a museum.

You don't really know him, but he likes to sit down next to you when he comes to the Bar. Why does he pick you to sit next to, of all people? As far as you can tell you and he have nothing in common.

He's told you the following facts many, *many* times: He is Croatian. He fishes coho salmon and brown trout off the shore of Lake Michigan with a trout line that he shoots out into the far distance with a fire extinguisher that makes a *pop* when he shoots the line out there and a claw hook that holds the line deep on the bottom of the lake so all the vertical hooks can descend into the water, already baited. Once the rig is set, he drinks slivovitz waiting for the coho. When he's not fishing his trout line, he's on the Des Plaines River fishing carp.

He says: When I catch the carp I like to keep them alive for a few days and let them swim in my bathtub that I fill with milk. That way I let the fish clear out all the mud from their mud veins and they will be that much more sweet when I eat them.

You've never fished in your life. You've never eaten carp soaked in milk.

One day he shows up to the Bar with a present for you. It's a Vargas pin-up.

He says: Do you know what this is?

He opens very carefully a bag with the picture of a naked woman who has yellow hair. Her legs are crossed chastely at the knees. You have some idea what it is but you're not willing to say.

Why is he showing this to you? Why is he coming so close? Doesn't he see that you and he have nothing in common?

He likes vodka.

You like tequila.

There's really no place in the middle where the two of you might meet. Yet he keeps trying. He says: You want to join me while I shoot out my trout line? I will bring the slivovitz and we will toast happy times.

You don't believe in happy times. You only believe in the very specific problems brought on by drinking: of how to pay for the next one and the one after that. Also, there is always the question of how to arrive and depart this godforsaken dump on your own terms. And how to make it home alive and in one piece, which is not so easy. The sidewalks are broken. The key to your apartment doesn't work very well. The other night you couldn't get in and so you slept curled up underneath a bush in the courtyard. It's okay. You were tired enough, so you slept, even while the raccoons went about their nocturnal business.

Anyway, these were the practicalities you were thinking about when he showed you the picture and then you promptly forgot these practicalities making it more likely you would think them again when you were done talking to him.

As you stare at the Vargas pin-up, the Croatian janitor quickly puts it back in the bag. He says: I can't be seen carrying this picture. It is a Vargas pin-up. Do you know what that means?

No, you tell him, I don't know what that means.

He says: It means, I will sell it to you for only two hundred and fifty dollars but I make that offer to you only because you are my friend.

With that he orders another round of drinks and while you think on the meaning of that price for that possibly stolen picture he raises his glass. He says: To the old happy times!

It's puzzling that he should put it this way because you've never spent a single happy time with him, or practically anyone else for that matter. You don't really know what a happy time is. You know what Happy Hour is but not happy time. Nevertheless, you raise your glass. What other choice do you have? The rules dictate it and so you say with him, touching his glass with yours, your pinky finger extended: *Prost*. Cheers. *Nostrovia*!

Inside, though, you are a chained tiger leaping against the bars of the cage.

Seventy

THE ALTAR

You show up at her home at lunchtime. You knock on her door and she greets you with a cold bottle of beer. She is already lit. You see it in her face, in her eyes. When she's drunk she has a certain way about her, and it's both irresistible and repellant. She is wearing a white satin nightgown. She walks you into the living room, which is filled with green plants and sunlight and...and what? And the perfervid smell of sex, you think. Are you coming from the Bar, she asks? I am, you say. She lies on the couch and lifts her gown exposing her nakedness and she asks you to pour beer on her belly and lick it off. Go ahead, she says. So you stand over her like an acolyte about to genuflect. You hold the cold bottle of beer directly above her belly button trying not to tremble. Please. Let it pour on me. You let a couple of drops fall and fill the shallows of her bellybutton. That's it, she says. You are good. Please. Go slow. Nice and slow.

Sixty-Nine

DRUNKEN BLINDNESS

You are here later than you should be and you've spent far too much money on drinks. You can't stand to go home. You can't stand to stay here. The snow is falling. It's a wet shitty snow and life is miserable. How long does it take for one minute to expire into the next? You try to calculate that for a while but the clamor in the crowded bar makes any type of calculation difficult. When the door opens and she steps in everyone turns to see who it is. Hat and coat veiled in snow she is every bit as beautiful as you remember her mother to have been when you first met her. Even though you are struck by her beauty, even though she is your teenage daughter: you put off for the longest possible moment any sign that you recognize her.

Sixty-Eight

WHEN HYDE PARK SWINGS UPON A HINGE

You wake up on 57th street beach while the febrile illumination of the moon works its magic trick and worms into the confines of the empty mescal bottle. The buildings in the distance stalk the land and your quiver of flaming arrows lies tossed in the pit. You can't decide whether you are a beached whale or a Jonah spit out upon the shore to start anew. That is when, after years of trying, you write a drunken ode to this neighborhood that has held you in its belly like a sacred seed all these years:

> *When Hyde Park swings upon a hinge*
> *And each and every mind is ajar*
> *Then the beaches like waves shall slowly swirl*
> *Rise themselves up and spit loudly upon the*
> *   gloomy lake*
> *And the earthlike clouds shall gather themselves*
> *   thickly*
> *And darkly spit rain into the star pocked sky*
> *And the buildings like bums shall weakly uproot*
> *   themselves*
> *And stumble penny poor and raving mad*
> *   through the streets*
> *Then crazy you and crazy me shall look madly*
> *   eye-to-eye*
> *And tremble firmly upon the ground*

As twisted tongue says to bent tooth: Dese are mad times Mistah Jones.
Bad times indeed.

Sixty-Seven

EULOGY FOR MOM

Your mother listened to you read the eulogy at your father's funeral. He slit his wrists and jumped off a boat. Two years later she listened to you eulogize your older brother, Matt. He died of a heart attack at forty-seven. Not more than a year after that you eulogized your younger brother, Nolan, who died an alcoholic. When your first daughter, Molly, died at the age of three of meningitis, your mother was there as you read the eulogy. When her own brother, Martin, died of a self-inflicted gunshot wound, she was there as well, and you eulogized him. Others called you "eulogizer-in-chief," but she took in each of your eulogies as if they were among the final missals of the Lord's Disciple; as if you yourself were one of the Lord's disciples and this were your missal—and because you were her son, because it was your missal, and because it was her Lord...she listened with eyes shining and breath bated. In each case, when you stepped down from the lectern she got up, staggered a bit, then hugged you. My son!

When she died seven years later after having lost her mind to Alzheimer's, they looked to you for something to say but you were so far gone on a bender you had nothing left to say. To any and all who would listen, and they were few indeed, you claimed you had been "hollowed out."

So, you sent her to the earth without epitaph or eulogy.

There was no Missal according to the book of You. There were no words said other than those by the priest who incanted what he had been trained and paid to incant. There was the small funeral cortege. The prayers at the cemetery, again, intoned by the priest according to ritual. The folded hands. The bowing heads. Then tossed in the dirt she was, and rightfully so, you thought. Is that a crow in the tree talking to me? Or is it she? We come. We go. We are here, then we are not. Here I am. Forget me not. You are forgotten. But not the things that you did to me. I won't forget the things that you rendered upon me, mom. I won't forget what you did to me when you thought I didn't know what was being done!

When the funeral was over, you dispatched to the Bar. You have been here ever since. Nowadays, to anyone at the bar who will listen—and they are fewer still—you say: My mom was the toughest person I ever knew. God, she was stoic and a drunk. It was fucking liberty when she died. She was cruel and a fucking bitch.

Sixty-Six

WHITE LIGHTNING

It was already hours into your drinking binge when he sat down next to you and told you the story of how he purchased a machete from a village market on the muddy banks of the upper Amazon and then marched into the jungle. He spoke for hours about the deprivations he suffered, the unrelenting biting flies, the lost tribe that took him in and taught him to speak their language; he explained their strange binary numerical system and how it consisted only of the numbers 1 and 2. He told of the way they managed time by always speaking in the single present tense, and how, therefore the past with its lost ancestors was always present as well. He routinely ate monkey roasted from the spit and he couldn't prove entirely he hadn't practiced cannibalism. He got drunk on the fermented saliva of tribal women. He told you how the jungle had broken him. He didn't expect to live much longer. Since he'd been back, he could only afford a small apartment in an SRO. He had taken up a hobby to help him deal with all that he'd seen. He said he collected the plaster casts of teeth. He found them in the dentist's office where he worked as a janitor. I have over twenty-five of them, he told you in strictest confidence. I keep them lined on a shelf. I find looking at people's teeth diverting. Sometimes I try to imagine all those teeth smiling and talking to me.

In truth, you won't remember what hobby it was he said he had, just as you won't remember a single thing he told you that night. His face seemed swollen because it was so intimately close to yours as he told you his tale and it was a shade of yellow as if he suffered from some jungle disease. He told you a story you said you would never forget. It was like white lightning what he said: it cleaved the drunken night. At one point you were laughing, and later you were still laughing. His story illuminated for a moment great interior clouds of bliss that you didn't know lived within you and then moments after he left the Bar the whole experience was gone. All you remember of it or of him is the uncomfortable feeling of teeth gnawing at the perimeter of your heart and how that made you long for a tall glass of black rum unmitigated by ice.

Sixty-Five

LARRY AND THE POSTAL CARRIER

You were a postal carrier and even though you haven't left the Bar in years you still call yourself a postal carrier. You say: Back in the day, I delivered the mail. I delivered it in all sorts of places. Those were the days, you sigh. You mention that there was a time in the sixties when you lived in Las Vegas and delivered the mail just a few blocks off the Strip. That was when the Sands Hotel was the biggest thing in town and then, because you couldn't stand the heat, and because you met this woman, Charley, who was a hippy chick, you headed up to San Francisco for drinking, for drugs and for mail. You liked to say: Mail was as much an evocation to me as drinking or drugs—and you used that word, 'evocation.' Mail took you to unexpected places. Then you tell, without further ado, the punch line that has become the story of your life: how you delivered the mail like a drunken god on the corner of Haight and Ashbury when Ginsberg and Ferlinghetti were kings. You knew Ferlinghetti and Ginsberg by name. You drank with them and you delivered their mail. Each of them received on a daily basis huge stacks of fan mail; Ginsberg more than Ferlinghetti. You and Charley are mentioned in one of Ferlinghetti's poems from his famous book *A Coney Island of the Mind*. You like to quote the specific line where you are discussed, a line written, some might point out, before you even knew Ferlinghetti: "Peacocks walked/under the night trees/in the lost moon/light." You quote the poem expressing where the line-breaks fall. You were one of the peacocks. You say: He was referring to me and my girl. But you say it like this, "Larry," meaning Lawrence Ferlinghetti, "referred to me and my girl as two pea-cocks. That's what we were, crazy in love and just crazy like two pea-cocks. We were that song the poet sang."

People keep waiting for the next part of the story. What happened next? At what magnificence did you tilt your saber? And what became of Charley? That's when, truly puzzled, you say, what do you mean what happened next? That was everything.

Sixty-Four

THE LUNCHEON

You have just one appointment today, a luncheon with your wife to talk through the details of how you're going to split up.

For the past few weeks you have been fairly certain that this luncheon, rather than closing a door, might lead to a new understanding. A golden understanding. In your mind you tell her this: I can change. This is not as big a problem as it seems. I want to participate in your and Missey's life. Let the past be the past but let the present and the future be decoupled from the past—let it go its own way. Let it go down whatever track we want to send it on.

You have been practicing this speech for some time. You stare at the bar-back mirror and you develop a series of sub-arguments: there is an array of positive-to-excellent reasons why you should stick together, and this should be the focus—rather than the negative past. You develop counterarguments just in case she digs in, adamant about the split. To this, you plan to say: There is no such thing as *must*. We make our own way. I can change. I am changing. I can beat this. While you sit at the bar you think about your teenage daughter, Missey. She needs you. Who knows what a permanent break might do to her? You imagine the three of you together again on a shopping junket: the three of you holding hands and skipping through a great arcade of glamorously illumined stores. You spin through some revolving doors and you're out again on Michigan Avenue. Just thinking about it swells your heart. Happy times await us, you want to tell your wife. We will step out onto the street, the three of us, and the sky will shine some blend of cornflower yellow and periwinkle blue and we will be like beautiful gods striding arm and arm down the boulevard.

When you think this last thought you are already lit. You are so fucking amazingly lit. You can't believe it.

To keep the ride going, you point with your finger to the bottle of Stoli behind the bar and nod your head, when the bartender asks: Another?

Sixty-Three

UMA UMA

You scrawled this on the back of a receipt given to you by the bartender. You wrote it down in a fevered moment because you thought it had value. Its value was as yet undetermined. But who knows, if you write a few more of these little poems and you compile them in a book, you might even win some fame as a poet. You write:

> *The Prayer of Uma Uma or How to Get There*
> *I am the The*
> *The that*
> *I am the This*
> *The Way*

After you write this little ditty, you tear the bar receipt from the pad you'd written it on, you open your wallet and, folding it carefully, you put it underneath a photograph from three years ago at a photobooth.

The photo is a black and white picture of the three of you. You don't even remember when or how the picture was taken nor do you know how the picture got in your wallet. But you were the only one of the three mugging for the camera. Your wife and your daughter appear grim and unhappy as if you had dragged them against their will into the photo booth. The moment that the black and white photograph records is lost from your own recollection, as is much of the relationship that it documents. So long my one and only family, you think, and goodbye.

In a day or two you will also forget ever having written this poem and sticking it in your wallet; you will even forget that after you wrote it you thought: If I write enough of these precious little ditties, who knows? Maybe I can get them published in a book. I might even earn some fame as a poet. Until then, you can't keep yourself from smiling at the crazy unexpected prospects that await you.

Sixty-Two

THE DREAM

In your dream your wife is cajoling you to go ahead and go with the woman. She says, Please go with her. She is yours. There is no reason to hold back. I have arranged a place for the two of you and now you shall be happy.

The woman in your dream is faceless, though you sense she is lovely. She is sitting on your lap wearing tight white pants, and when your wife tells you to take her to the place that she has arranged the woman is thrilled. Come, she seems to say by the way she leans into your body and then begins to pull—come, let's go. Let's begin our time together.

You feel happy about this change of events, you feel thrilled by your wife's generosity, but as you leave with the girl in the white pants you come to understand (and how you come to understand this, your dream does not say, unless there is a voice-over): From this moment forth your relationship with the woman known as your wife shall be over forever. It is to be understood that never again will you have so much as a conversation with her.

In your dream the irrepressible beauty is pulling you away, to the bed no doubt, but even as you're pulled away, you look at your quickly departing wife and you want to tell her, you want to say: This cannot be true. I do not want to spend the rest of my life never able to talk to you again. You are the one I love to talk to; you are the one I need to talk to. But the lovely arm of that haunting beauty pulls and off you go to that place your wife has arranged for the two of you.

In reality it happened very much like this: You met a woman at the bar. You allowed her to tug on your arm, and before you knew it you were out of the bar and on the street and headed to her apartment as fast as your legs could carry you. What happened at the apartment that night, you will never forget. You keep it in your heart even as it displaced the precious gift of your wife's conversation.

Leave, your wife said, when she found out about the affair with the young woman. She said, quite calmly, with a calm that took your breath away: This and all this that we have shared between us as companions in life (she used those exact words) is over. We, you and I, are done. You can have your fancy woman from the bar, or anyone else for that matter. But I'm done with you. What's more, and I probably don't need to say this, but you've become a drunk and you no longer belong to me. Go back to the place that's claimed you. Go back to the Bar.

Sixty-One

MARTINI

1. A martini is a crystalline snowcapped mountain that you can ski with your eyes closed.

2. The winter air is scented with the smell of pine and your hair is blown back and your eyes are squinting against all the hurt that you've ever known.

3. You proceed zigging and zagging down the slope to the sea-washed margins of the glass where the salt-brined olives await and dolphins swim in a sad pink light.

4. God, you feel like a giant!

5. God!

Sixty

TWO DEATHS FORETOLD: YOURS, AND THE WEATHERMAN'S

You sit at the bar every afternoon and avidly watch the local weatherman not knowing that you and he will die at exactly the same time, three years from now.

You and the bartender watch the weatherman go through his routine—it's part of your routine. When it's snowing out, the weatherman tells you with satellite images; when it's 75 and cloudless with five-mile-per-hour winds, he tells you that this weather will last for the next three days and then it will either spike or collapse depending on what's blowing in from the northwest. He will tell you when you can no longer bear the heat—that the heat-wave is due to an *El Niño* effect—and it will continue for the next seven days. He will also point out that we are in the middle of a three-year drought, and that lake levels are at an all-time low; he will advise those who have breathing issues to stay indoors. While he tells you these truths, you drink your martini. You and the bartender talk about the weatherman as if he is a friend that is right here with you. I like his suit today, the bartender might say. Or you might point out: Who else but a local weatherman can get away with wearing such ties? But the weatherman's voice, his gestures, his hair combover, his gentle sense of humor are all so pleasurably avuncular. It's one of the great amenities of this place, you think, that the bartender understands the importance of keeping the television tuned to the local and not the national weather station.

One day in the not so distant future, let's say in nine-hundred-and-seventy-two days, it will come to pass that this very weatherman will be at the ninth hole at the Kemper Golf course for a benefit. In the days leading up to the benefit he will predict thunderstorms and a plague of hail and yet he will defy his own predictions and show up on the golf course because the benefit is to raise money for leukemia and his own son suffered and died of that dreaded disease. The benefit at the ninth hole, the son with leukemia—all this will come out later in the news when, as he predicted, a tremendous thunderstorm blew in from the northwest; but the news accounts will also say how even our very own weatherman had lost his life, killed by that thing his charts couldn't contain: bad weather. The weatherman was striding across the golf green with putter in hand when a bolt of lightning hit him.

But you don't know this yet, nor does the bartender, nor even the weatherman. Everyone is still alive now and overwhelmed by the quotidian: you by your worries how you're going to pay for your next drink, the bartender by his worries how he's going to make rent, and the weatherman by his worries over his terminally ill son.

Nor do you know that at the very instant the weatherman is struck by lightning, you too shall be struck as though by some internal electrical storm which shall lead to stroke, and with the hail battering your window, you will breathe your last. You and the weatherman will die together, he on the golf green and you alone and asleep in your bed, and it will be several days before your dead body is discovered in the wreckage of your apartment. During that period of time—from the moment you die until the moment you are discovered—the bartender will gossip with anyone and everyone who walks through the bar and he will talk about the weatherman with whom he has become obsessed. Can you believe, the bartender will say, that the weatherman was struck down by lightning? The weatherman couldn't even avoid his own death by storm! And how many times has the great Trevino been struck, but never once killed! Maybe it was his outrageous ties that tempted Zeus to strike him down with a thunderbolt.

It goes without saying that the bartender won't even notice that you stopped showing up at the bar. Nor will he know why you have stopped, and when he discovers why: that you had a stroke and that you had lived in pecuniary tenuousness, he will hardly care. He has only room in his heart for the tragic death of the weatherman.

Nevertheless, today is a typical day and you and the bartender are lost in the quotidian. You are drinking your martini; he's drinking a beer out of a glass. You smile with the bartender at the silver lightning bolt on the weatherman's red tie; you comment on his messy combover.

It's such a mop!

Yep, that's the way with these local guys, the bartender says in agreement.

At commercial break you gaze out the window of the bar and you see in the distant sky a long shapely V of Canada geese. They are flying high in an azure blue broken up by giant puffs of white clouds. It is the longest V of Canada geese you have ever seen. It is so long a V that at some point you simply lose its thread.

Fifty-Nine

THE LAND OF GUILT

For years you inhabited the land of guilt. You were raised in the Catholic Church; you were a ringer of the bells at the moment of transubstantiation; you were a confessor of sins at the confessional, and you said your *Hail Mary*s and *Glory Be*s, and you trod a narrow path of righteousness. But you were a glorious sinner when no one was looking, and for these transgressions you offered no apology or explanation. It was how you were made, you thought, though you felt you couldn't let that be known. You started drink at an early age and hated that you loved it and you loved that you hated it but you drank when no one was looking. And you drank. God how you loved to get smashed on vodka on weekends away at the home up in the pine woods. The home is gone, as are the family members you hid from while you got smashed. And now, all alone and out in the open, you still drink vodka. It reminds you of those days of youth drinking when no one was looking, drinking when it was a goddamned sin which you weren't going to confess, drinking because that's how the Good Lord made you— nice and fucked up.

Fifty-Eight

THE LAST REMAINING STORIES

You have become in all your years at the Bar a collection of well-told stories. Those who visit on occasion like to talk about all the stories of all the characters at the Bar and you have become one of them and thus you have sharpened your stories. I will be the entertainment for anyone who steps through the door. Just as zoogoers visit the apes and look for some recognition in Zolo the great ape, so too, they look to me. I am in effect an animal at the zoo so that the casual bar-goer who wishes to be entertained by one of the regulars may be entertained and find in my stories a sense of recognition.

But what are those stories? You sit there tonight at the bar and try to do an accounting of your entire collection of well-worn tales. You sort them out by funny, sad, and nostalgic. Then re-sort them by a different order: sad, nostalgic, and funny. Then you consider how many stories you actually have and while you sit there only three come to mind and you realize for the first time that all these years all you are and all you have are these three stories, and you've discovered that you can tell each one funny, sad, and nostalgic—so that gives you a total of nine tales to tell, but it all boils down to this: the story of how you met her, the story of how she left you (her hand rising and waving as she stepped into a taxi—see you! and then she was gone as the cab disappeared into a pink light) and the ever-growing story (more sad and nostalgic than funny) of how you've coped here at this bar with the unraveled meaning of those first two stories.

The one story you haven't yet told but that consumes your every moment is the story of when she'll one day walk again through these bar doors and see you as a man and not some animal at the zoo—the moment when she sees you as a human and, touching your hand, pulls you away. Come, she says, enough of your tired stories. Come let's find out who you really are.

Fifty-Seven

NOTHING

You don't want to do anything and this is the place you are most allowed to do that. You don't even want to drink all that much but you recognize that drinking is the minimum activity required in the Bar so you order a glass of beer and you nurse it and as you approach the midway point in your glass of beer you ask the bartender to replenish the coolness of the drink and so he drops a few ice cubes and then as this melts down you sip and ask for a few more cubes then sip as it melts and in this way you can pass a pleasurable ninety minutes or so with hardly spending any money on booze and you deploy as little effort drinking as you can.

You don't want to do anything. You never wanted to do anything. You didn't want to be anyone either. You never had goals or ambitions or hopes—what for? We will all die soon enough. Better to sit back and observe the grand old show.

You have always identified with the trees. You are a tree, you like to think. You could stay in the same spot forever and not do a thing. You could shake when the wind blows or stand frigid in a winter cold snap. You exist to watch the clouds tumble overhead like slow motion circus performers. And, you say, there's the cloud shaped like an elephant, and there's the camel. Yes, you can sit all day long waiting for just one cloud to resemble the trapeze artist. Is that it? you ask yourself. The way it slopes down like an artist dangling from her knees from the trapeze bar? But no, maybe not.

You like sitting in the Bar watching the light change during the afternoon: the way the pink light falls into this place pooling in corners of the bar as the sun moves to the west. You like the different people who come into this place. You watch them come and go. The crowds ebb and flow, as does the volume in the place. You go with the flow. You find your seat. You sit. You drink as little as possible without drawing the ire of the bartender. You choose this place because no one who knows you knows that this is where you come and so you can't be found.

Time is a river, you think, or a creek or a harbor—some type of water, you are convinced, and without using your oars or your pole to push you out of places where you're snagged you just let your boat drift on the current of time. You patiently wait and see where it will take you: bumping along some bank and through a splendid glade of spectral greenness or over a rush of rapids. When I was a boy, you think to yourself, I was a tree and I have always been a tree. I can't decide if I am a willow tree on the muddy shore or if I am a piece of driftwood floating along. It is okay to let yourself go; to be nothing; to harbor no ambition; to be emptied of want; to be completely thoughtless and at peace.

Here they don't mind what you do so long as you buy a beer once in a while—you do as little as possible and in that way you have discovered the deep reservoir of time that goes nowhere.

You sit at the Bar and think: When I was a boy I sat on the bank of the river with nothing to do but fish.

Fifty-Six

LEPRECHAUN

It's Saint Paddy's Day and you make the extraordinary decision to wear your father's kilt to the Bar, plus a shiny green cardboard hat. After drinking a fifth of Jameson commingled intermittently with pints of Guinness you notice in the wee bottom of your glass a redheaded leprechaun riding a purple pony through shamrock-green fields cut by a burbling brook. Behold! He rears back on the reins and jumps off his purple pony. He finds himself in a clover patch and there the leprechaun sets about the daunting task of counting the petals of clover looking for a four-leafer. As you sit there watching him (the purple pony cropping the clover with its green muzzle) you feel it's the most beautiful image—the most stunningly beautiful thing you've ever seen in your life. And you start to cry.

Fifty-Five

BEACON

The new bartender, Heather, who shows up every Wednesday and Friday evening wearing false eyelashes, has caused you to switch slightly your routine. You discover that you like drinking beer and watching her work even better than you like just drinking beer and watching any of the other bartenders work. Each time she lifts her long-curled eyelash to ask if you need another drink another shutter on your soul gets raised and pulled out of place and then her eyes stare into yours sending a beacon of light to dark places in the hole that haven't seen illumination in a very long time.

Fifty-Four

ARTIST

You are an obsessive. Can we say that you are penniless, which would be the truth, or that you live in a garret, which also happens to be the truth, or that you will never emerge into view as an artist? Of course there was your breakdown, your failed shock therapy, and later you became sequestered: a hermit. Some of these biographical facts are glossed over because you are too accustomed to them to notice. You now sit at the Bar drinking, and as far as your money situation will allow, you drink vodka and orange juice.

Anyway, months before this shock therapy and all this other stuff happened that led to your sequestration as a literal hermit, well out of the blue you decided you should design dresses. Do you remember that? Dresses...and not just any dress would do, but a hundred dresses to match a thought you had.

You worked rapidly, drafting and cutting patterns out of paper. You hired a seamstress, instructing exactly how to make this dress or that. You worked by exact specification. You picked the fabric. White for a wedding. You preferred silk to rayon though you could virtually afford neither and how you afforded the seamstress no one knows. Within a month the seamstress had produced dozens of dresses to match what? The dress of your imagination, or the dream that would embody it? No girl was found to fill the dresses until you put an ad out for models. A teenager from the local high school answered the ad. She showed up in your apartment and tried each dress on while you snapped photographs.

In the bright afternoon light you watched through the shutter of the camera the harsh beauty of her plain skin; too much to bear. You used her as long as the money lasted and then it was over. Then came the long nights of wandering that you couldn't account for, the raving, and the threats to blow up the Sears Tower, and the holding of the knife to your mother's throat until you were subdued, shocked, and sequestered.

Your mother is dead now and with your small inheritance you live out your days as meagerly as possible. You are a hermit, and when not a hermit you sit here at the Old Home, you call it, which is really just the Bar.

You sit there drinking your orange juice and vodka and you tell people that there were a hundred dresses she had worn for you as you snapped her picture and when she left you hung the dresses on a rack and covered them in layers of red acrylic paint that you smeared with your hands until the dresses stuck together and when they had dried it was as if they had become frozen in a rictus of death like sides of beef in a slaughterhouse.

Fifty-Three

THE FACES

You watch them come into the Bar all day long. The ebb and flow of faces: some of these people are regulars like you and so they bear a passing resemblance, but many of them are unknown and unfamiliar. Who are all of these people and what are they doing? At certain moments they seem inscrutable beyond recognition. You have been watching them. You've been following their gestures carefully trying to make out what it all means. What can all these people packed into the Bar together on any given night possibly mean? What does it mean? Perhaps it—and by extension each one of them—means nothing at all. It doesn't help that you can probe them with language, for often speaking to these people only confuses matters and makes them seem even more faceless and inscrutable than ever. But no matter...You have another vodka and watch the great pantomime. You tell people you meet that you are from a pig farm in Iowa. They laugh, or they say, really? You are filled with unspeakable emotion. In reality you are inviolate and singular. You are a holy flower lit from within. You know deep in your heart that you have been sent from Neptune's tenebrous moon, Triton, to bear witness and report back.

Fifty-Two

THE CRUMB

It is midday and you occupy your habitual spot at the Bar. The red stool you sit on has become your stool. There are other stools in the bar and some of them are occupied but at this hour—the afternoon lull—you can count on finding your stool unoccupied and so you occupy it. You sit there sipping your beer. You stare at the TV and order a bowl of chowder. When the chowder comes you crumble crackers into it and you talk about how the soup is better than usual today and that is, the bartender has told you, because they scraped the bottom of the pot for you. After you finish the soup the bartender removes your bowl, your napkin, your silverware. He wipes down the bar and pours you another beer, then he walks to the other end of the bar and watches TV. From there you find yourself untethered and lost to the doldrums of the afternoon. Your sails grow slack and the going is slow. You try focusing on the television but frankly you can't make sense of the talking faces. There are competing and unclear voices drifting through your head. You can almost hear your wife mentioning your name. Without inflection or valence—she says it as if she were trying to wake you from a long sleep. When you open your eyes you find you haven't been sleeping at all. In fact, you have been here at the bar drinking a beer trying to get through the doldrums of the day. That's when you notice a small ant pushing a small cracker crumb down the bar in front of you. You watch for the longest time the ant push the crumb. Humans are just smart ants, you think, but ants are smarter. The ant is so small, and the crumb by contrast is relatively large, and that is when it occurs to you that you are just like the ant except that you are an ant pushing the cracker crumb of your soul.

Fifty-One

THE WRITER

You and everyone else at the Bar referred to him as the writer. By calling him the writer you each implicitly understood that he was a great writer and you implied this by a slightly hushed reverential tone: The writer, do you think he will come into the bar today?

You each had read his book. There was only one book and it only took an afternoon to read but it was a great book. As any of the gospels are short, yet great, so too was his book. It told a simple tale of what it is like to be a brother to a gifted drunk who dies tragically out of revenge for an unpaid gambling debt. It was written in an incantatory voice reminiscent of a Presbyterian minister. Most of his life the writer had lived in disguise as a relatively ordinary person: he had been a teacher at the university and a scholar of the Great Books. It wasn't until his seventh decade—in the winter of his life—that he sat down to pen his tale, which he described as only penning nighttime stories he told his children to put them to sleep. You tried to imagine it while you sat at the bar—the writer, not yet a writer, putting his too-hot pen (set glowing by the gods) to paper and penning the first lines of his masterpiece. To hold in your hand the power of a perfect sentence—even then, sitting at the bar, dreaming of one day becoming a writer, you could think of no more glorious thing to happen in a life. And when he set his pen down to the paper and wrote down the first words: *In our family, there was no clear line between religion and fly fishing*...he must have known from the very first that he had hit upon a brilliant proposition and you can feel in the writing itself the writerly joy of that good luck. The cadence of the language was exact and forward-leaning; the voice spoke with authority yet it was athletic and trim. What's more, the metaphorical resonance of two fisherman brothers growing up in the first decades of the twentieth century alongside the unspoiled Big Blackfoot River in outback Montana was as rich as any in the gospels—throw in gambling, drinking, a beautiful wayward girl, and the scowling disappointment of a bewildered father, and he had concocted a book that would last the ages. No more would he be a teacher of the classics at the university— he had entered, with his brief book, the firmament of greats...

Will he come into the Bar today? Will the great writer grace us with his presence? Each of you waited patiently—surely, he must show up soon, he lives only across the street in that modest apartment building, and while you waited you talked about it: How was it possible for one common man so late in life to write a song that sang of your own goddamned lost and doomed and father-damned waywardness? How was it possible to be so doomed, and sing?

Fifty

THE LAST SIGHTING OF THE GRAND MISANTHROPE

He wrote prolifically: days, months, years on end. It was amazing to anyone who followed him how he was able to produce such volume from day to day. He seemed lit from within by an unquenchable fire. He was filled with invective, which he called holier than prayer. He spit rage and trembled the page with portraits of idiots who were his contemporaries, and was called courageous when he pointed out how they were allowed to run rampant: unchecked, in fact. His words were the subject of joy to millions who followed them through the ether.

Worse yet were the unknown idiots he shared the buses and trains with each morning and evening: the stink and humanity of these fools caused him to fill pages and pages with words for which he won not only rewards but the renown of acolytes who gathered around him like bugs warming themselves near the light of his fame.

Of course, these acolytes became the subject of his poems and plays.

How he reviled and abused them in print: pointed out their stupidities, their lack of originality, and yet they still came knocking at his door to see some aspect of themselves manifest in his work and to hear the great man tell them something about themselves they desperately needed to hear.

And then one day apropos of nothing the great writer stopped writing. His daily habit of stepping up to the page and saying what people thought but never said merely changed into the habit of not doing it.

No crisis or cause was ever ascertained. He hadn't, as some speculated, burnt out, charring his inner core with the white-hot flame of invective.

Was it pornography, like Larkin? Or the lost love of a woman? Or disappointment that stopped him? When asked why he ceased writing he merely said: "I suppose it was like a faucet. One day I noticed it had been running and I quite simply turned off the spigot."

They followed him for years afterward. His muteness became the subject of their articles, the articles became books, and the books became objects of contention in a long running debate. They speculated if some tic threw the great man off his game. How could an artist who had so much magma in his core stop at the top of his form? The acolytes in their insatiable need tracked the writer down and seemed to find him no matter where he ended up: on an island in the Gulf of Mexico repairing boats for a few years; later, slouched over a bar on a seven-year binge in the Village where he raved on and on about the lunatics. They even found him repairing car tires in a garage on 87th street long after they'd given him up for lost or dead. That was more than twenty years ago.

The moment of his last sighting was at the Bar on the South Side of Chicago. After this he would dissolve from history. Two or three times he had come in. You saw him, a silhouette against the pink light of afternoon that was pouring in through the front window. You were certain it was him, the writer. You had read his every book. You had read much of the commentary since he went mute. You had followed the debate of his silence. There he sat, the writer. You had thought of asking him a question or two but you held back and watched him out of the corner of your eye. You tried to keep up with him, going beer for beer, but you fell behind: the torrent of his alcoholic pace was too much. Taciturn, focused— he smoked a cigar as he drank. You knew him only from publicity photos yet you could see how he had aged. At one point he turned to you and ordered you a brandy. Shall we have a drink? he asked. It's a lonely enough afternoon as it is: nice to have a bit of company. You lifted glasses with him and said cheers and then you asked: Aren't you the writer who stopped?

To which he replied: I smoke a cigar because I like to smoke and I never stopped writing. Only now it just gets written here in my head. Why share it with those shit-fucks?

From this moment forward, he escapes the public record. What became of him, no one yet knows. But you...forever afterward, now you can say: I shared a brandy with the great misanthrope!

Forty-Nine

EYE-MAGNET

You step into the Bar and do a little stutter step. They stick their eyes upon you. You pull their eyeballs off like cockleburs and throw them to the ground. You saunter over to your spot. Even though you're a dying animal rotting on animal bones, you are given your daily elixir— a stein of Miller Genuine Draft—and for an hour or two you are a radiant angel smiling through skeleton teeth!

Forty-Eight

THE FILCHING TONGUE

There were the shadows cast in the hollows of the eye sockets over-cliffed by the up-furrowed brow over which her black bangs dangled, and there was the sparkle of life itself peeping out of her witnessing eye, which prior to lifting its gaze to you had been muted by droning interior thought, and then there was that nose instinctively pointed like a sight-line that focused the eyes' gaze upon you. It was this look of inquisitive alertness that made you feel alone and isolated, and yet part of a great humanity of equally alone and unreachable isolates.

When you sat down at the bar next to her she pushed her hair from her face then grabbed your head, and, putting her drunken face near yours, slipped her wet tongue into the open seashell of your mouth and she kissed you. In your startlement, she broke away laughing.

Forty-Seven

THE VOICE

Sometimes when the jukebox plays you hear not only the music that the jukebox plays but also a secret voice speaking to you. It speaks to you in truth. You watch a man unfold a dollar and feed the bill into the machine and he plays whatever music he likes and then another person will drop some coins into the jukebox playing their favorite set of songs and through the night the jukebox rolls. There's not a song on the box you haven't heard a thousand times and yet there is from time to time a moment when the jukebox speaks only to you in a secret language. There is the music and there are the lyrics all of which you know by heart and you will even find yourself tapping your foot or singing along—but then there is also that voice coming from the music that no one else hears—it speaks only to you and during these moments you are happier than you know how to express. Whether it's Tom Petty or Billy Holiday or Cat Stevens doesn't matter—what matters is the voice speaking to you, and that voice tells you that everything you ever thought about anyone—everything you have ever felt—it is all true and everyone is safe and good because from your lap grows a red rose that drops its petals on your blue jeans. How could it be otherwise? And this magical, glorious voice—God, how it sings the truth.

Forty-Six

THE HACKING

It is true that today is payday and you know long before you wake up that as soon as you cash your check you are headed over to the Bar. You are tired of nursing your drinks—to stretch the night. You are tired of smiling and hoping that the guy next to you whom you have bought drinks for in the past will look upon you in your moment of crisis and buy you a schnapps. You are tired of living the truth of what it means to be broke all the time, so tonight when you get your check and cash it you decide to splurge. Why not? Work is hell. You feel trapped, hemmed in. I'm a man, you say to yourself, not some caged monkey that exists only so the zoo-goer can poke at me with his stick. And yet that's what work has become. You're a mailroom clerk in a large office. In other words, you're the monkey. Your boss and countless others in your organization are the zoo-goers poking you with their sticks, watching how high you can jump. They like to watch you smile and prance so they poke you some more. You are tired of jumping. You want relief. You want to say, in perfect freedom: I am a man and this is what I am. The cash gives you the freedom and as a man you saunter into the bar. You sit down and you start to buy a round of drinks. Why not? You only live once. Tonight, the joke is on them—the ones with the sticks. Let's laugh and drink to that, you say, and cheers. You lift your glass to the fellowship of drinkers at the bar. You even buy all the bartenders drinks, then tip them generously. Why do you tip them generously?

Because they did such a good job pouring their own drinks. You order another round of drinks because that thought you just had is a funny thought. What was the thought? You don't know because you can't remember. That's the problem with always being poked by a stick. It's killing your memory. The more you get poked the harder it is to remember. What's your telephone number? I forget. What's your name? I don't know, why are you asking? Do you know a woman named Mary? Mmm...I don't know. She says she's your wife. Now that you mention it, her name sounds familiar. She's been calling all night asking if you're here. What did you tell her? We told her the truth. And what's the truth? We told her you're not here. Well if I am here, I sure as hell can't remember ever coming here. How did I get here? Who am I? What am I? Let's have another round, you say.

And so it goes through the night until, coming through the bar door is a Fury, embodied as a woman you once loved but you forgot about. What is love? What was love? Why all the fuss about love?

The Fury slams down on your head with a violent hacking gesture causing you to scream out in pain. You are temporarily blinded. You can taste blood in your mouth. Have you completely bitten through your tongue? Down comes that hacking action again and again the temporary blinding and more blood. You see it in a blur the arm coming down as it hits you again.

You sense an alien feral hunger coming from that embodiment of fury that resembles a woman you once loved—and then you feel it again as the hacking comes down, and then you feel the most painful hurt you have ever experienced. You feel your ear getting violently twisted as she pulls you off the barstool, dragging you by the collar and calling you names that don't seem to apply: You fucking animal! You pig, she screams at you. How many times do I have to call this place before you realize it's time to come home? And even as she drags you out the door you stare back into the glowing bar, and you think to yourself even though it comes out as a scream: I had my freedom in there tonight! I lived like a knight at a roundtable of knights! I lived in a circle of truth and plentitude. I am not wrong for living how I live. I am righteous and I would not change a thing.

Forty-Five

THE OBSCENE GESTURE

It's inexplicable to you why you feel the sudden urge to turn to the guy sitting next to you at the bar and point your finger as if it were a gun to his forehead and pull the trigger and kill him. You're dead, you want to tell him, if I ever see you in this bar again. It is inexplicable why you feel this sudden urge; it is even more inexplicable when you enact the gesture your mind imagines. You stand up from your bar stool and with a level of aggression that you've never before experienced you stand, and, without screaming, you make the violent gesture, which by its symbolic nature and what it represents is an obscene gesture.

Earlier in the day you had been in the botanical gardens. You had found the Japanese garden whose gravel had been carefully raked and an autumn oak leaf had fallen on the raking. The oak leaf was mottled orange with brown spots and there was a bit of dark green around the curling edge and it stirred gently in the pink light. You wanted to be that oak leaf. It had fallen in the most peaceful place you had ever seen. You didn't hold your breath so much as stop breathing. You looked out toward a koi pond and saw a slight breeze ripple the surface of the koi pond. In the distance you could not see but you heard the sound of geese and you thought the words "Uma Uma" without thinking why.

Now you are here in the bar and no sooner do you pull the trigger then you regret everything you are—everything leading up to this moment that made you pull the trigger, and when he starts beating you over the head with a violence and hurt you have never before experienced all you do is cower beneath the blows until two barmen and this gentleman you have accosted drag you kicking and screaming out of the bar and toss you like garbage as far as they can into the street where a passing city bus just misses crushing you.

Forty-Four

TOAD MAN

He slept at night and dreamt of frogs and woke in the morning croaking. He stepped onto *terra firma* a toad and became the most toad-like man ever to sit at the Bar, where he sat crouched down, eyes bulging, and when he turned to you he lifted his glass and croaked, I am the most mysterious creature known to man: unloved by lass or lad, I look the toad; I sit here nonetheless and drink my crème de menthe and soda; I dream of green sticky things, or so it's rumored, and from my hollows I reverberate, for those who ask, that hallowed word: ribbit.

Forty-Three

GAZELLE

She shows up at the bar slack and loose and slightly out of breath as if she had just finished a sprint. Her cheeks are red and there are tiny little droplets of sweat-dew on her brow and indeed she is a jogger. She has just finished running. She steps into the Bar and stands next to you. When you turn to her you're struck how like a hunted animal she looks. When you ask her name she says, Giselle, whereupon you say, Gazelle? That makes her laugh and you laugh too. You buy her a drink. You sit down, clink your glasses and say cheers. She looks you in the eye and smiles and for a moment you walk and then crawl across red-hot volcanic coals to touch there in the just beyond the distant pink-stained shore of infinity.

Suddenly she says she must go. You stand up and thank her for her attention. Then she steps away and is gone. You never see her again. Not as long as you live.

Forty-Two

THE READER OF J. M. SYNGE

How deep the well of J. M. Synge? Quite deep, presumably, by how carefully you stare into it. What is it you see staring into the still pool of his plays his sonorous Irish voices not causing a stir to ripple the surface? Perhaps you hear the low querling of the old guard muttering in the way they did when you were a boy in the turf-tufted land of your Irish youth. You sit in the radiant pink light of afternoon day after day in the middle room of the Bar so far from home your only companions are gin martinis with pickled onions and the dark memory dance of ancestral sounds rising from the bottom of that tar-dark well.

Forty-One

THE PANTHER

Her love is a black panther with spots. You've seen the spots. They are shaped like brown eyes and they are visible beneath the black fur of the panther. You recognize implicitly that the panther is her love. How could it be otherwise? The panther lives in the forest of your soul. Who else could possibly inhabit the forest of your soul? You sit at the Bar, you close your eyes and you are content to know that lurking in the forest of your soul is a black panther with eyes the shape of almonds. That's another way you know the panther is her love. Her eyes are almond-shaped. You see those eyes peeping out from beneath the fur.

The forest of your soul is a wooded place. It's a jungle. Getting around the jungle of your soul is a real bitch sometimes, especially when you are hunting for the black panther. You know she's there in the tall grass that fills the clearing. You see the top of the grass rustle. You are a warrior hunting her love. You call the panther by name. You call it Julie. Hello Julie in the tall grass in the clearing of the jungle of my heart. I come in peace, you say, tipping your glass of whiskey back. The days of war are behind me. Please, let the lamb that is my heart sleep side by side in the tall grass with the black panther that is the almond eye of your love.

Forty

THE TURK

Midget Mike steps into the bar and sits down next to you. He's neither a midget nor is his name Mike but that's what he's called. The reasons for this appellation are lost to time but you figure odds are good you'd be correct if you said his name referred to how he was hung. Midget Mike sits next to you. He orders a stein of beer and he says, How goes it, Joking Joe? Your name isn't Joe. It's Pete, but because you like to call him Midget Mike in such a joking manner, he now has taken to calling you Joking Joe. You order a stein of beer and the two of you clink glasses. Have you seen the Turk? he asks because, apparently the Turk owes him money. The Turk is not from Turkey, nor is he Middle-Eastern in appearance. His real name is Bob and he's from a pig farm in rural Iowa but he's known as The Turk because he famously burned his face and neck when a turkey he'd been deep-frying in peanut oil exploded on him. His face is an unbearable mass of scar tissue. When he returned to the Bar after a year of reconstructive surgery he immediately became dubbed the Turk. The three of you raised steins and toasted his return. Here's mud in your eye you said. All for one, one for all, Midget Mike affirmed. Here, here, mumbled the Turk. He drinks vodka now and breathes through a hole in his throat. He says he's not from a pig farm, though he did a six-month stint at a pig farm, once. He says his real name isn't even Bob. Then what is it? I'm certainly not telling you two fools, he says. And then he says, quite inexplicably and apropos of nothing at all: The tail wags the dog my friend. The tail wags the dog.

Thirty-Nine

REMEMBRANCE

You sit at the Bar and you are stunned at how effectively you have stilled your own thought. Great slabs of time seem to have fallen away like heat shields from a rocket and there is no accounting for what happened to you during those lost years of childhood but the disappearance of that time and those things done to you is directly related to this ability you have cultivated at the Bar. There is the stopping of thought, you think to yourself, and that is a hugely difficult thing to accomplish, but harder yet is the stopping of the images and the babbling voices that speak to you from places that you have yet to locate. If you could only locate where those voices are coming from, then you might be able to root them out and silence them. On your sojourns away from time you descend into the dark space and you sit there not as if you were a breathing being, but as if you were a non-breathing, non-animate being. You sit still as stone in the dark space of your soul and wait. Flickering images light up like the aurora borealis, and a burble of voices. There is the sound. You hear it again—a tremendous noise that completely rattles you down in the dark. It goes *Pinggg*. And then after a very long time you hear it again.

You follow the gloved hand up into the shadowed darkness that the arm disappears into, and then you see it: the jawline—pale white, sweaty—and the eye that is neither blue nor blue-green but a dusky shade of gray.

The eye belongs to him, as does the hand gripping the can of Meister Bräu. You see it now as you saw it then. The hand. The beer can. The eye that did such nasty things to you. You take a swipe at it after all these years to return the blow, but on it continues in the dark cellar: *Pinggg.* It continues obliviously.

Thirty-Eight

WINDBAG

The apprehension slowly dawns on you over the years that others perceive you as a windbag. You may be lacking in social acuity, but gradually you perceive that you bore the shit out of your interlocutors, whose eyes frequently glaze over, or flash into barely obscured terror when they realize you've cornered them. Nevertheless, you carry on in your 'windy suspirations,' as you call them. It doesn't matter whether what you say bores them to tears or not. What matters is that you have someone to talk to, or to talk at.

The bartender pours you a drink. An unsuspecting person sits next to you. The bartender pours that person a drink, then he walks to the other end of the bar. He's heard it all before. He knows the routine. He waits and watches as the neophyte falls prey.

You speak in joke and when you don't speak in joke you speak in truisms and when you aren't speaking in truisms you revert to clichés and when you run out of clichés you repeat the same old stories you have always repeated. There aren't many in your bag and they're all well-worn tales. Your mouth keeps moving and the words keep tumbling out but in truth you don't know what the hell you are saying. What can any of this gibberish possibly mean? You can hardly follow any of it yourself. You stare in a sort of wonder that this motor and drivetrain of words, your brain and your mouth, is capable of such profuse locution. You feel that you yourself are a dark plinth of towering silence and whistling solitude and yet the words swirl around you like a tremendous whirling storm kicking up all the leaves and debris in its lifting embrace as it turns into a spinning cyclone. I am at the still center of that cyclone, you think to yourself, even as you produce the prodigious wind that causes it—and this truth is the only thing you don't know how to put word to.

Thirty-Seven

THE INTERLOCUTOR

Meanwhile, as you speak, you eye your interlocutor, who happens to be caught—button-holed—by you as you deliver yet another of your drunken stem-winders. Unlike you, he is too socially conscious to ever go on speaking such trifling nonsense while the person he talks to grows so obviously bored.

You can see it by his posture and body language, the way he pulls away from you. All he wants to do is drink his beer and be left alone but he's either too kind or too ill-at-ease to tell you to shut up so you rattle on at him and as you do so you look at him through the prism of your words and you know something about him that even he hasn't yet figured out how to express. You see that he is nothing more than a solitary and towering plinth comprised of dust that one day very soon the wind shall blow away as easily as this: poof.

Thirty-Six

THE GROOM

You sit there day after day and you move with deliberate slowness. You are heavy and sloth-like but your gesture, your every movement, is calculated ballet. You reach with incredible slowness for the drink on the varnished bar-top. The elapse of time goes by, one tick and then another, and your hand is still reaching as if across an incredible distance for the drink. It is in the deliberate gesture that you have learned to still time, and in this great pool of slow-moving time your desire swims like a great green fish in a murky aquarium with nowhere to go.

The window in the room, colored by twilight into a dim rosiness, is half open, and its white drapery, caught in the same light, is sucked out of the window and then breathed back in by the quiet draft of this late afternoon. You reach for your glass, and with incredible slowness you bring the drink towards your mouth. What is the rush? you think. The drapery is heaving to and fro as the bedroom of your childhood memories breathes while you nap. You take a sip of your vodka and you let it pool in the bottom of your mouth just beneath your tongue, and then you let your tongue swim around like that green fish in the aquarium. You breathe to the rhythm of the breathing room of your childhood nap and set the glass down on the glistening bar and when it touches the varnished wood you remove your hand from the glass and reach around to your back pocket where you touch the plastic tines of your comb. You pull the comb out of your pocket and without the slightest bit of haste you bring the comb to your brow and, staring into the childhood mirror of your memory, you pull a strand of hair back from your forehead and put it in place where it belongs on top of your head, and as you bring your arm back around to your pocket you insert the comb. You let your arm fall in a heavy but deliberate gesture to the side of your lap, and your fingers drop loose. At that moment you gulp down your vodka.

Thirty-Five

THE COIN

You sit on your barstool and after long, deep, ruminative cogitation you finally discover the answer to the complex question: Am I a man or am I a jerk? Just as a coin has two faces, a head and a tail, so too are you like a coin. And the answer is that you are both. As to what face comes up most often when randomly flipped, well that depends on who's flipping the coin, or so you reason. For instance, if it's your ex-wife flipping the coin, then likely what most often comes up is 'jerk,' except when you're appealing to her to stop applying pressure on you for alimony payments. If it's your estranged daughter who's flipping the coin—well, she's not even returning your phone calls, much less flipping your coin, so there's no way to tell with her. If it's your parents or siblings who are doing the flipping—well, hard to say: they're all dead except for one who is a drunken asshole living in a small town on the Jersey Shore. Closer to home, if it's the bartender who's flipping the coin then the answer is more likely fifty-fifty man/jerk depending on how long you have to wait for a drink or how generously he pours. To be fair, more often than not you try to be a man to him, but he sees that part of you also as jerk. To your boss who makes you do every dirty shit-fuck task he doesn't want to do because he sees you as nothing more than an animal that he has to pay—well to him, the side that most often comes up is man. I am a man, you seek to confirm in his presence, not an animal. But whenever you try this tactic—which you have been trying for years—he says, no, you're not a man. You're just some stupid asshole that I have to pay too much money to, and even as the asswipe that you know that you are, you aren't worth shit. Ah, you think to yourself, one day I'm going to kill that bastard. On the other hand, as long as you drink three beers an hour and sit in the bar four hours a day, and as long as your job continues to pay enough for that, you'll likely just continue to appeal to his better angels. But to this question of the coin, what is a coin? A coin is an object whose only value is related to how it works in a social system of currency. Outside that social system the same coin has no value. It is a trinket: something to gather dust and be forgotten. You don't want to become a trinket to those with whom you relate, so you make sure they understand that you cannot be so easily dismissed. As to the question: Who are my social relations and how am I thereby valued? You look around you at the drunken derelicts scattered about this place, and you frown at the truth, so close to home, that sociability is a burden not everyone can bear. You sit there a while longer thinking. Why all this thinking? Why am I sitting on a barstool thinking about any of this at all? I came here to have a good time and to forget. A moment later it occurs to you that in some ways it wasn't the fault of your ex-wife that the whole marriage went to hell. It was your fault every step of the way, beginning with the first step. The fact is, you asked her to marry you and when she said no, you arm-twisted her for years until she finally complied. But why did you want to marry her? You were never in love with her. You were only in love once in your life, and it was with a different woman whose name was Mary. You'll never forget that love as long as you live, nor will you ever forget that you lacked the courage to express that love, nor will you ever forget that with Mary too you were always, always a jerk because if she, your only true love, wasn't going to see you as a man, you wanted her to at least see you as a jerk she couldn't ignore. In that way, you wanted her to feel the full weight and value of your currency in her hand.

Thirty-Four

YOUR SONG

She is a breathy female voice that at its sonic center is
girlish with a southern twang and she is a voice singing
like a white bird twisting in pink twilight splendor above
a jangling acoustic guitar that her naked fingers pluck
and strum. She sings songs you know because you keep
playing them, and her voice has grown so familiar since
you discovered it that you now recognize it as a voice—a
specifically female and girlish voice—that's directed at
you. Her voice is intimately close, and since it's directed
at you, you imagine her eyes also directed at you. You've
seen pictures of her in the ether and by virtue of how she
looks and the sound of her voice you have come to
associate her with Mary, a woman you love with
heartbreaking intensity. It doesn't need to be said that
you are the only person who would ever draw this
association between the singer, a southern pop star, and
Mary, because in truth they look and sound nothing
alike, but such are the mystical properties of love: they
give you insight. When you are sitting at the Bar and you
hear her voice come over the jukebox you try not to grow
annoyed at the people around you who disregard her
voice entirely. They don't have the same insight you do.
You try to find yourself a little private space at the bar.
You cup your hand to your ear to capture the sound of
her voice, which you have come privately to call 'Mary's
voice.' You say to yourself: Mary is trying to tell me
something that is surely seductive and urgent and tinged
with regret, but it's impossible to hear her with all the

racket in this place. You strain to listen to what her voice is telling you. And then you hear it and it's the most beautiful thing you have ever heard. She's saying, Let me touch you for a while where you most need to be touched. She's asking your permission, and then her naked fingers pluck and jangle the guitar strings. She sees you sitting there at the Bar with your hands cupped over your ears and she is asking: May I touch you like that once more?

But you are touching me, Mary, you try to explain. And you point with your own naked finger: you're touching me right here. You're touching the cold jagged edge of my frozen and fucked up heart with your tender and loving song. Just as she breaks into chorus, the guy next to you spills his beer and because you are so filled with the joy of her touch you hug him with tears in your eyes and buy him another beer.

Thirty-Three

THE PAUSE

Here's one story you like to tell at the Bar...

Before she left me, you say. You pause a moment for emphasis. Then it occurs to you in the lull that is in that pause that there was a moment before she left when neither you nor she knew or expected that she would leave you. That is the moment you always seek to reclaim: the moment or moments before it even occurred to her that it was time to leave. Then there was the moment when jokingly she said: this was never meant to be. That happened one afternoon in the white sheets of her bed when you had come and surprised her with a bouquet of roses and she let you into her bedroom and she received you by removing her clothes for you and the two of you laid out in the clean white sheets of her bed merging your two nakednesses and you were like a hunter suddenly lying with the beast you had hunted and you asked forgiveness in the pink afternoon light of the fading sun for stalking her love and even though you were the hunter and she was the hunted she gave to you freely everything she had and when she was done giving the two of you lie in the tangle of sheets and that's when she said while she was laughing: this was never meant to be.

That was the moment she stepped over the fence to escape, and you didn't yet know she had stepped over the fence, and she pranced away and was gone long before you even realized. At this moment, the pause in your confession has lasted long enough, and you say what you have said so many times in the years since— before she left me, the bitch.

Thirty-Two

PEE

You are a boy even though you are a man and you have spent your whole life peeing as a boy even though as a man you have mostly pissed beer.

When you haven't peed in the alleys or against the brick wall or against the dumpsters or into the sewer blocked from view by a parked car; when you haven't peed against a tree or a fence post or an electrical pole; when you haven't peed out a window onto a bush or off a roof onto the pedestrians far below; when you haven't peed into outhouse holes or reeking porta-potty-cesspits at the tail end of a summer's heat wave, then you have peed in countless bars against countless urinals.

You have peed against *quality* Republic Manufactured urinals while the crows outside *cawed*. You have peed in wall-mounted urinals high and low. You have stood in cleated urinals and have pissed to your heart's content. You have peed into stainless steel troughs, shoulder-to-shoulder with others, dicks out in a brotherhood of steamy piss. You have peed in the solitude of single-occupant toilets. You have peed in a crowded john, your feet sticking to the tile floor. You have peed staring at condom machines wondering what it all means: *Rugged 'n Ready*, *Passion Plus*, *Her Pleasure*, *Ultimate Skin Tight*, and *Arouse*. You have melted countless pink urinal cakes. You have been one with perfect aim and you have been one to completely miss the mark, until slowly regaining your balance you find the bull's-eye. You have stood there waiting for the pee to come, wondering when it would, and the pee has come when you hoped it wouldn't, and when you stepped back into the bar the bartender and everyone else in the bar noted: Ah, so he's pissed himself again.

To let the pee pour forth from you with its sonic hiss like water pressed from a bellow and squirted against the porcelain bowl is to feel a slight but sublime pleasure whose regular recurrence has yet to mitigate the joy of relief.

And every once in a while, there's bonus night like tonight when they put asparagus in the soup and you can sooner than you think possible smell that astringent, vegetal smell in your piss. It reminds you of your boyhood in the country when you used to piss in the roadside ditches and in the springtime you often noticed while you pissed the green wild asparagus growing there.

Thirty-One

FLOWER BUD

In the jeweled light of a spring night you spy the purple unopened buds of magnolias tipped in white and pink and you realize all of a sudden that you are going to die, that death is inevitable and without mercy.

> *The thick-fingered petals of the magnolias reach out to me in the night, they stir my senses awake. In the morning sodden and rotted on the ground, I, sotted, trod their pink flower petals under foot.*

That your death announces itself in the mode of doggerel is your great epiphany, or at least it's great enough to make you smile. There is a raccoon rummaging in the bush whose fur is mottled by molt, and there is the alarm of a passing ambulance that reminds you of the sound of the crying baby that was once your daughter long before you became estranged from her and her mother—it reminds you also of death, but you are on your way home from the Bar and you are drunk and you are feeling grand even if you are going to die. Because you realize that though the magnolias bloom tonight and fall tomorrow you shall be granted at least one more sacred day to throw open your arms like petals to the sun, to the stars, to all that is broken and dirty and to all that is sweet and clean. And tomorrow you promise you will awake fresh from this fever dream and live again no matter what chaos and rot ensues.

Thirty

ETERNALLY LIT

You had seen once long ago when you were an eighth grader the Eternal Flame of JFK at Arlington National Cemetery and you marveled at the idea that a flame might flicker eternally. Even then you joked with your comrades about the concept of getting eternally lit. There must be some switch, you reasoned, that if you could only find it and flick it on, it would keep you lit until the end of your days.

Of course by now you have forgotten about the Eternal Flame; you have forgotten about those old comrades, and you have forgotten that it had once been a passionate dream of yours to find that switch. Once in a while an old friend will discover you sitting at the Bar. There will be a flicker of recognition and then it will snuff itself out as you try to remember who the person is and how you once knew him. If he speaks to you and he says: Remember me? If he says, we stood together years ago and pissed on the Eternal Flame, you will say, of course I remember you. How could I forget? In your mind, at least, that's what you're saying: How can I forget you? But all he hears is an incomprehensible grunt that sounds like: I don't know who you are or why you're invading my space but get the fuck away from me before I kill you. You order another drink from the bartender because just before you were interrupted by this idiot you had seen in the darkness what looked like that elusive mythical switch you had spent your whole life searching for, the switch that once turned on would keep you permanently lit without the need to ever order another fucking drink from this asshole bartender again so long as you live.

Twenty-Nine

THE DOG

The bartender whose name today is Heather is the one you have come to love above all others. You sometimes wonder: If you hadn't always seen her here while you were drunk, would you love her as passionately as you do. In other words, would you love her as much if you had run into her in the pink light of the public square while she was carrying groceries and chased by an ill-begotten dog that followed her everywhere? Yes. I would love her even more than that ill-begotten dog that trots after her loves her. But who cares about that shit. You will never see her outside the confines of this bar, and frankly you don't care to. You have her right where you want her. You lay the money down on the bar. She pulls a handle and the beer over-foams the stein.

Twenty-Eight

THE PROSPECTIVE FUNERAL

You know you're going to die, and though you have come to think of yourself as reviled on earth by all who know you (with the possible exception of the bartender whom you keep in business), little do you know that on the day you die you shall cause heart-rending in friends and family, many of whom you once loved more dearly than words but who you have one by one abandoned, and though you anticipate—in fact expect—a pauper's burial because you have managed nothing better than a head of cabbage in your fridge and a photo album of pictures long ago snapped, yet the papers shall fill columns of ink talking about who you were and all you had done, and after your wake the bar shall lock its doors to strangers and through the night Irish fiddles and drums shall play while the funereal crowd gathers to hoist a long night's round in your honor. And impromptu speeches will be made, and they will talk about how the papers and writings you have scattered to the four winds shall be collected and bound into a book so that your ideas will be given their rightful due, and your long-estranged daughter shall show up at your funeral and, in your honor, she will drink for three days into a blackout stupor, and after the funeral she will only have a vague recollection of how she got pregnant, and will not remember all the things she had said about you. But while you sit there drinking today you will look at yourself in the bar-back mirror and you will reflect that it is a tragedy you have lost touch with her, but a benign comedy that as a result you will never know what she really thinks. It can go any way, you think: pauper's burial, or the party of your dreams where the fiddles play and the drinks spill onto the floor and the bartenders collect their ripe harvest of gratuity. Yes, it can go either way, but first they will all have to wait for you to die.

Twenty-Seven

THE GOD

When you think of the gods you yawn. What else is there to say? If there is something more that needs be said on the subject, your voice joined to the din of the garrulous chorus is probably not needed. So, in pertinence to all things god, you yawn. Then there is the bartender, Heather. She's a god. Why has no one written a Biblical tome about her? Why isn't there a gospel dedicated to Heather? If there were such a gospel it would tell how she is the god that keeps men's asses planted to their barstool day after day. She is the god that keeps men like you coming into this holy sanctuary to go through the daily ritual of losing moments of your day, as if the chain on a bike sprocket slipped and lost a few turns. In other words, you ask for a martini, she pours it, you pay her, and there is this slippage in the chain of time that occurs that is hard to explain; and with this slippage comes glimpses of timeless pink-lit rooms where the white dogs of eternity sleep. But this isn't about explaining. In fact, the Gospel of Heather says that you will receive your martini that she pours as if it were a holy elixir, a sweet benediction. And as you sip that elixir she has poured for you, you think: she is the alpha and the omega. And the bar is an altar and her body is Christ's body and the Buddha's body and Marilyn Monroe's body all wrapped up in one, and you want to pull the red ribbons off her and eat her slowly, deliberately, like you eat the salt-brined gin-soaked olives that roll down to your mouth from the cool wet lips of your martini glass.

Twenty-Six

THE DOSE

How much vodka have you consumed since she left you seven years ago? She was in your life for fifteen years, and in the early years you were a social drinker. That's what you tell people. What is a social drinker? Well, that's a tricky definition. A social drinker is someone who drinks in society. And for a while you did most of your drinking in society. You didn't let drinking encroach on the home front. While at home you were dry, and when you wanted a drink you hugged your wife. But slowly, over time, the social drinking migrated home, and you drank with your wife by your side, and you called it social drinking because she was always there even though she herself wasn't a drinker. You sat and got lit with her by your side, and when she went off to bed you continued to get lit, and that's when it started to become asocial drinking, or as she sometimes called it when you stumbled into the bedroom drunk: asshole drinking. Because she called it asshole drinking, because she called you asshole, because you were an asshole—what the hell? you thought. And that's when the vodka started.

What is vodka? Well that's a tricky question too. Vodka is a clear, slightly sweet grain alcohol that comes in a bottle, usually a very pretty bottle, though the type of bottle hardly matters to you anymore. Vodka is also a state of mind. That's the thing you have come to understand. Vodka is a ridiculously sublime state of mind. It is a blurred light shimmering just above the dark green and distant Latvian ridge of your deepest memory. It is the droning sound of a wasp trapped in a can that you hear with your molars. It is a joke whose punch line is endless. And it is a yes. It is always a yes. Would you like another vodka, the bartender asks? Yes, you say, staring at your empty glass and then staring at her. Yes, please.

Twenty-Five

TATTERED CAPE OF WAR

You unfold then unfurl then wave high overhead on a stick the metaphorical cape that signifies the brokenness of everything you know. It is a long pink cape and it is tattered and it is patched and it is torn and it has been shot through by bullets during the long drawn-out war that is the saga of your life. You point lovingly to the cape, which is stained pink because you have kept it wrapped tightly like a tourniquet around your heart, and you wonder what to do with it. It was once a beautiful cape, but now there are far too many holes to mend, and all these tatters can't be untattered...it looks as vainglorious and battle-worn as that flag they flew above Iwo Jima. And that gives you the idea. You throw caution to the wind and you strap on your combat gear and with metaphorical flag of brokenness and victory in hand you advance one more time up the hill, drink by drink—and that's when they hear you shouting from the end of the bar, screaming as loud as your lungs can scream: You think you can ignore me, motherfuckers? You think you can replace everything that I stand for? You think you can take this battle flag from me? Bring it on, motherfuckers! Come on! Bring it on!

Twenty-Four

THE MATADOR AND HIS WINE AND HIS AUDIENCE

When your brother was still alive, you watched him drink like a holy monster and you promised never to step in his way. He was the god that sat at the still center of the Bar; he was the black hole of gravitation that held the focus of the place; he was the pupil at the dilating heart of the eye. But more to the point with a glass of wine in hand, he was a bullfighter, a grand matador. He stood at the center of the bullring that is the Bar. He held the cape of drunkenness in his hands. He taunted the bull on the bottle of Sangre Del Toro. You watched night after night in the empty coliseum of the Bar as he brought the cape close to his body, gave it a shake and taunted the bull. On its first charge he would stumble, he couldn't get out of the way and he took a goring to the thigh, but he pressed on with his next drink and his next; holding and shaking the cape of drunkenness tempting the charging bull to gore him again. As the bull gored him through the night, your brother would let out a groan that sounded something like blame. It was a groan filled with anger and hatred—and it was directed at all the idiots out there. He would manage to hold the center of the ring and out would come another bull, and another—until he was caught in the mix of a bull-rush and a melee—and a coterie of clowns would gallop to his aid and while he was twisting on the ground in his bull-cape, they would bring him back to his feet and order him another glass of Sangre Del Toro, and on through the night the goring by bull would continue until he would fall from his stool and piss himself and try to get up but collapse in a mumbling angry heap. And you would let him lie there, night after night, letting the bar door slam behind you— letting him, the grand matador of monstrous consumption, figure out how to make his own way home.

Twenty-Three

THE RIVER

It is unusually crowded for a Saturday afternoon, and when no one is looking you dip your foot into the muddy river. You order another beer from the bartender and then, because no one is looking, you decide to start fishing in the muddy river. They'll never notice, you think. They're too busy talking, getting drunk. And while you sit there all afternoon it occurs to you that this is who you are: you are a boy and a man sitting on the muddy bank of the river with a fishing pole in hand. You are the fishing pole, you are the line that you hold between your fingers as the current pulls and tugs at the weight attached at the other end. You are the worm on the hook that still wriggles in the green murk of the river—it wriggles as it must to get off the hook, but this afternoon, which is an eternal afternoon, you imagine that it wriggles for the sole purpose of enticing a fish to take a bite at it and instead of getting the worm, the fish enhooks itself on the pointed barb. You are the wriggling worm saying come hither to the carp and bullheads that swim lazily in the slow current and the deep pools of the river, and you are the eye of the fish that sees the wriggling worms and that obeys the fish-brain that says: take it. Take it now.

On the radio is a tune that is the perfect tune for a hot day in the shade of the river-bank. You are that tune coming out of the plastic box. You are the voice of the disc jockey who brings order to the afternoon in a slow, pleasant cadence befitting an afternoon like this. You are the cloud of gnats. You are the buzzing mosquito. You are the biting fly. You are everything you are, and not everything you are, and you bring all of that to the bank of this river that flows unnoticed along the footboards of the bar.

Twenty-Two

THE LETTING GO

If time were a mountain...if the time you have yet to live were a mountain...

In the distance are the mountains and they rise up improbably and unscalably before you...

If time were a mountain, you think to yourself, I would like to turn my back on the mountain. After all, you think, I am not an alpinist. To turn your back on the mountain has always been a dream—to let go of the future. Just as a shadowed man, clinging with a finger-hold to the cliff, finally decides to let go of the rock face and fall freely into the pink-lit canyon below, wherever that takes him—this is a perennial dream of yours that you have given yourself up to in a disorderly and endless spree of drink. You can't remember if today is yesterday or tomorrow and you don't care. You sit in the bar. You drink your beer.

You order another beer.

You drink your beer.

You order another beer.

You drink your beer.

You order another beer.

You drink your beer.

You order another beer.

You drink your beer.

You drink your beer.

You drink your beer.

You drink your beer.

You drink your beer.

Beer. Beer. Beer.

And always you are falling, falling into the glow of the light below.

Twenty-One

THE THUMB

You are so drunk you put your thumb in your mouth and you suck it and when beer doesn't come from it you take the beer bottle that is in your other hand and you throw it against the wall and you start crying and you piss your pants and you want someone to come quick and spank you and tell you you've been bad but that everything will be OK and all will be forgiven and then you want that person to find your pacifier which has fallen somewhere on the dirty bar floor. You want that person to clean it off by rubbing it on their shirt and then you want them to stick it back into your mouth so that huffing and puffing in short gasping sighs you can pull yourself together again—or at least pull yourself together in such a way that you can order yourself another huh huh another huh another huh huh another bottle of beer please.

Twenty

THE LAST KNOWN ADDRESS

You try to remember your last address, which is hardly different than remembering your high school locker combination, or the password to your bank account. But you don't have a bank account any more so there's no need to remember that password, or the name of your first dog (which was a dachshund called Schnitzel), or the name of your mother. Your mother...what was her name? Oh, who knows, and who the hell cares? Nevertheless, you sit there at the Bar for the longest time not only trying to remember her maiden name but trying to remember her actual first name. You believe her first name must be Kurtz. Or Schnitzel or Amy or Rose...What is a rose? A rose is a red flower with pretty petals and a thorny stem. Though your mother was neither red nor pretty, she was thorny as hell. She was a goddamned briar patch. It made your insides bleed just to look at her. And when she died everyone looked to you—you, of all people—they all looked to you to stand up to the podium and say something nice. There was nothing at all nice that could be said about her. You can't even remember her name, much less anything that was nice. But her eyes...those you remember. Oh yes. You will never forget her wicked, hateful eyes. They could be red as a rose and thorny. They had your number and insofar as they were your only home, you had theirs: 428 Willow Street.

Nineteen

THE CURLER'S STONE

After the great letting go there was the intense scramble to find you. Friends and family searched every known location for you. Your records were checked. The police were called and a missing person's claim was filed. But you were lying so low the searchlight never caught its own reflection in your eye. In reality, all you did was change bars to this place. You like to enter it from the backdoor so no one from the street can see you coming or going. You walk past the kitchen and turn into the bar and take your seat. They know you here and you have asked them to call you Bill. Hi Bill, they say. What can we get you today? Or more often than not they just pour you a stein of beer from the tap. There you sit watching the dew collect on your stein of beer and before long you order another and then another. At some point you open the local paper and you see your picture displayed. You are missing. They are looking for you. If anyone should find you they should report it to the police. This is the number they should call. Should you report yourself, you wonder? You drink your beer and watch a bit of TV while you consider it. Today at two in the afternoon they are playing women's curling. How perfectly they slide on the ice before they release the heavy stone that glides on the ice in the wake of the other womens' dusting brooms. Oh, how you would like to be that heavy stone—pushed with such delicacy and grace by the lovely lady—and then how you'd like your path cleared for you while you glide on toward whatever target you are destined to hit.

You look down at the paper and see a picture of yourself with the word "Missing" written above it. Where'd they get that mug shot of you? Why are they looking for you? Can't they see that you have let go? It is time for them to do what you have done. It is time for them to let go of you—gracefully and with intent, like that curler letting go the stone as it slides, guided by its own momentum across the ice to either peter out alone or collide with another stone. Either way, so be it.

Eighteen

THE HOME

You were a giant—a monster of vitality. As a boy you vowed: nothing in half-measure, and you stormed the beaches of your youth like a soldier taking the cliffs from the enemy. I will climb every cliff that falls between me and my destiny; I will part every curtain that falls like a veil between my eyes and truth; I will stare unblinkingly into the eyes of anyone who opposes my advancement, and push them aside.

You strummed a guitar in a rock band. You rode your bike across the Pampas; you watched the bullfights and learned from a matador how to hold a cape like a *subalterno*. You swam with movie stars off the coast at Cannes and, pick-axe in hand, you climbed Mont Blanc in July. In the pink light, you laid in a field of clover with a girl named Cindy. She wore your Rolex on her wrist and her father owned a house in Big Sur on a cliff overlooking the sea. You read the great poets. You wore a blue beret. You smoked Gitanes. You flew in a private jet with a diplomat to Cape Horn and sailed on a wooden ship to the iceberged shoals of Antarctica. You smoked hashish under a glass. You smoked crack cocaine in Chicago with a blues singer named Cadillac Sam. You smoked Cuban cigars and Jamaican weed with a reggae star whose name you can't remember though he told you that while traveling in Scotland he went by the name of Paul and that's what you called him until you were so high you didn't know what to call him, and then you called him Pauly. In Mexico you drank what your idols drank: mescal. And leaning up against a palm tree, you shot heroin while the black frigate birds with stiff wings sailed high in the blue ozone. And you wondered why you numericized yourself as six, tattooing the Roman numeral VI in sepia ink on your left shoulder, wondered why, even though you also realized it was the most truthful thing that could be said of you.

Once you followed behind a bloodhound and chased fox. Once you followed behind a hog and discovered Oregon white truffles in the fallen leaves of an old growth rain forest that was ancient as eons and lost from time and you claimed a spot in a hollow for your grave and then you went on your way. One day you were blown wildly off course by trade winds that cradled you like a dream in the hand of thought over a cup of tea.

You lost your wife. You lost your job. You slipped through the cracks of the economy. You were fifty-two years old and without prospect. Your daughter was already an alcoholic and, inexplicably, extradition charges were lodged against you for your arrest in Panama for murder. Yes, a man had died. Yes, you had been in his presence when he died. No, it was not murder. It was a coincidence, the same way that you were watching Verdi's *Requiem* performed by the Chicago Symphony Orchestra with Claudio Abaddo at the helm when some bluehair dropped dead in front of you—during the Requiem! They didn't even stop the performance while the paramedics silently removed him. So too were those murder charges, so to speak: the Requiem was playing, and he died, but it was a coincidence. Ever since you have been on the lam. What other choice did you have? It was you against the law, and the law would only win if you stuck around. That's when you changed your name, then you changed it again, and then you changed it yet again until you found a name that fit and that sounded to your ears like con man and nice guy all rolled up in one. You called yourself Billy.

You remember the first moment you stepped into the Bar. It was a nothing place. It was a hole. It was a cipher and a zero that added up to disappearance. It was the greatest, the most fabulous place you ever saw, and you saw it none too soon. It was a place you could dominate with your stories until the end of your days and still nobody would listen or care. When you opened the doors it spoke to you in a language only you heard, and you heard it deep in your bones. It said, Welcome Home, Billy! Welcome home!

Seventeen

WHAT DOES IT MEAN

What does it mean that you met a woman at a bowling alley and then two weeks later the two of you drove in your convertible across the country with the top down rain or shine (because the top was broken); that you drove until you hit the coast of California and then drove north along the coast up through Canada into Alaska until you arrived, several weeks later, in Juneau, and only then, because winter was already setting in, did you trade your car in for a pick-up truck? What does it mean that you stayed all winter on the North Slope in something that was half log cabin, half trailer home, and that the two of you adopted a dog that you swore was part wolf, and that she named Lucky? Is that what the two of you were back then? Lucky? What does it mean that she broke ice every morning with a hatchet and melted it down for the day's water? What does it mean that the two of you built a smokehouse and that you hung brined sockeye salmon from a wire? What does it mean that you both built a sauna that lasted you most of the winter but burnt down in March? What does it mean that she taught you cribbage while the two of you sweated in the sauna naked? What does it mean that you conceived your daughter on the last night of the year beneath the Aurora Borealis while the two of you laughed and wept with joy, and that in September when you were back home with your new job you named your daughter Borea in memory of that night? Or what does it mean that she taught you how to conjugate verbs in

French? Or that she talked a trapper down six dollars on a .375 Winchester that was the best rifle you ever owned, or that when you saw a grizzly bear sniffing around your smokehouse that you didn't have the courage to shoot because it was too beautiful a thing to see? What does it mean that all of this happened more than thirty years ago and that only you and she know? What does it mean that you haven't talked to her in years? What does it mean that your daughter, Borea, now twenty-nine, is on a troubled course, and that you have been here at the Bar so long now that you have come to believe that all of it means nothing?

Sixteen

YOUR VICTORY

They wanted too much from you. You had to be born ready to compete for a corporate job. Always you had to stay on the straight and narrow. Your parents, concerned of your natural waywardness and worried that you might not be corporate stuff, stuffed you with Ritalin to keep you even-keeled and participatory. It was the ultimate 'smile' drug. I know you're not happy, and you know you're not happy, but there's no reason the world should ever see that you're not happy. A smile is a harbinger of success. A yes is always preferred to a no, except when a no is preferred. Please learn one from the other and act appropriately.

They wanted nothing for you other than happiness. They knew life was long and fraught with pitfalls, secret traps, weights you didn't know you had that would tip the scales either disproportionately in your favor or against it, but regardless of how the scales tilted your mission was to comply, to be a team player: to take the white that was you and blend it to the white that was them. And so you went like an automaton: you went from school, to corporate job, to consultancy, to beautiful wife and child, and you never raised the red banner of revolt because to comply was to be happy. But no one ever discussed the alternative. What if you were to say no? What if you said, I will not go another step? What if, on a whim, you simply stopped going to work? What if you stopped paying your bills and let your credit rating go to hell? What if you chose instead a path of least resistance, which for you has always been drink?

What if you allowed the brewing company to reach their long hand into your brain to find the switch that, once activated, would allow you endlessly to say no? Leave me the fuck alone. I wish to follow the slide as long as I can, and after that see what happens.

What if you say the truth: they wanted too much from you. Every single goddamned one of them wanted too much. But how can that be, you think, when you don't want anything at all? That's when, lifting your empty stein, you say to the bartender, I'll take another.

Fifteen

THE DOUBLE

Every time you came to a fork in the road you chose the path less traveled. There have been many forks and there have been many roads. But the roads slowly became pathways, and the pathways became rutted trails in a wilderness to nowhere, and there you stood in the pink sunshine of a green glade looking around you wondering how to get the hell out of here. Now you sit at the Bar drinking your doppelbock, and you ponder your doppelganger, who must have taken every pathway you didn't choose.

Where did that lead him? Your pathway that seemed destined for promise led to a spot of light in the middle of nowhere. You travelled the pathway with enthusiasm until you had followed it too far and realized it was a trick: a hall of mirrors. And when you tried to exit the funhouse it was no longer fun, because you discovered there was no exit. What does all this mean? Well the question remains: if you had followed the other fork, as your doppelganger must have, where would you be right now? In other words, where is your doppelganger this very moment, as you sit in the Bar drinking your dopplebock? Is he drinking a bock beer in a bar on the other end of town? Is it possible, you wonder, that he's taken the world by storm—that he too had a wife and a daughter, but that they are together, the three of them, living happily and spinning through the revolving doors on Michigan Avenue, arms laden with packages? Is he sitting in the house that you long ago lost? Is he loving the woman who long ago left you? Is he speaking to the daughter who has ceased all contact with you? What is his name? Why does he haunt you? Why won't he follow the pathway back and come join you for a drink, to tell you at least once what that other life was like? He can come as the crow flies—for surely, you're not that far apart. Who knows—it may only be as simple as this: You drink vast amounts of beer, and he probably only drinks gin martinis on Fridays. You have let go and are falling into the pink light and into the nether spaces down below while he is running like hell, screaming to get let out of the madhouse.

Fourteen

QUIETUDE

It's hard to realize that you are meaningless and that no one needs you. It's even harder to realize this day after day. You order a beer from the bartender. You set your dollar on the bar. He pours your beer and sets it on a coaster. He picks up your dollar and steps away to the cash register and rings it up, then steps to the other end of the bar. You wish you didn't know what his name is. You wish you didn't know where he grew up. You wish you didn't know what he thought about everything the two of you watched on the television—that way you would be able to ask him: What is your name? Where are you from? What do you think of this show? And thereby the two of you would be able to start up a conversation, and with conversation you might watch a moment or two of the afternoon slip by without notice. As it is, you know everything you need to know about the bartender and he knows everything he needs to know about you. You order another beer. He pours it. You lay the dollar down on the bar. He sets your beer on the coaster then rings you up and steps away. You sit in the bar at the quiet hour between one and two in the afternoon. It's just the two of you. You may as well be alone. It is so quiet you can hear your breath. Inside your breath you can hear your thoughts. Your thoughts are quiet, but if you listen carefully you can hear the noise in the quietude of your thought. It comes through like a discordant screaming up from some deep well of emptiness.

Thirteen

THE LETTER

You haven't written a letter in years and so this afternoon at the Bar when you ask to borrow a sheet of paper and a pen you find yourself puzzled by the strange feel of the pen in your hand and by the rusty almost-awkward way the pen scrapes across the paper. After you attempt to write a few words you set the pen down. The words don't look right. Nothing is as it should be. You take a sip of beer and stare out the window at the passing traffic and have a memory of how years ago you once wrote so fluidly you could fill pages of paper with your writing. If letters and words were horses, you ran them like a cavalry up and down the page. The horses left their tracks in the mud and in the green muck of the fields and when you crossed the white-hot dunes you saw the tracing of their hooves in the sand. And in the snow forest where you sat high in the saddle looking into a clearing where the ravens gathered around the body of a fallen deer or the red birds flitted out of the green pine trees to peck for seed in the snow, you saw the tracings of their movements left behind in the white snow; all this your writing expressed. Your handwriting was never pretty—but it was astonishing: the speed and fluidity with which you wrote seemed burned into the calligraphy that you laid down on sheets and reams of paper. That was when you wanted to be a writer. That was when the world seemed bursting with possibility. That was when all the convoluted minutiae of the inexpressible world seemed on the cusp of being said.

You scratch the letter I. You pause, take a sip of beer. You stare out the window. You squint at what you've written, then you add a W and an A, an N and a T. You pause and set your pen down.

You are done. Finished.

Twelve

THE DYING

This is why you're dying: because you're fallible. When you feel what you know to be true: that there is something inside of you that will kill you in three weeks, you say: I am dying not only because I am fallible. I am dying because I am *fucking fallible*.

You knew it would come to something. You anticipated that it would come to something. You spent a good many idle hours dwelling on just how it would announce itself. My death, you used to say when you were so drunk that you were talking as rationally as a mathematician describing some elaborate but infallible conjecture talks—my death will announce itself. You said this not only as if you were a mathematician, but as if the saying were some dramatic piece of news. My death will *announce* itself.

But you knew there was nothing new about it. Death happened, as did life, and death was as prosaic and meaningless as life was. There was death all around you. Folks lined up and down the bar dying, rotting on the stick of their tired bones. Those who weren't dying, were fornicating. That's what you hoped at least—that all of these young beautiful children (and that's what you called them, *my children*)—that all of these young beautiful children were fucking. I hope that they are fucking. They better be.

Now your death announces itself and you are unprepared for the announcement. You feel suddenly as if you had made some grave mistake—or a wide assortment of small mistakes that piece by piece led you inexorably to a spot you don't want to be in: this bar, this death announcing itself. Who am I? You are garlanded in daffodils, and an unstoppered god of joy wells inexplicably in your heart. I am me and all of this stuff, and now very shortly, I will be only this stuff. That is when you want to call your daughter and tell her finally who you have become. You want to say: I am just the blank empty stuff, the dust that collects on the windowsill and captures the pink light of the passing sun, and soon I will be only that. You want to tell her that with all your soul. But she is gone. Where she has gone—you have no clue. How to find her is even more mysterious. Now there is hurt where there was joy. Soon you will be stuff. Soon. You turn to the bartender and, slapping the bar to get his attention, you say: Hey! Buddy! I'll take another beer.

Eleven

THE ANCHOR

An old friend shows up to the Bar and he notices you right away. He reaches out his hand without hesitation and he looks you in the eye and he seems genuinely interested and happy to see you. Is it possible at this late stage, for anyone in the world not only to recognize me in this godforsaken place but to show genuine interest and happiness in that recognition? What does he see in me, you wonder? Does he see a man charred out by the white-hot fires of truth? Does he see a man who stepped aside and trod a different path—a path not of righteousness, but a path that said: I will go my way no matter what, while everyone I ever knew in the world goes theirs, because they're too scared to step outside the ring?

They told me my way led to hell and ruin, and I told them I would go and find out for them—they could contact me in twenty if I were still alive to tell the tale. Is he come to hear from me the truth of what all these years have added up to? Is he come to ask me to give him the coin I said I would repay after I went on my twenty-year walkabout from my room to the Bar and back?

I knew I'd find you here, he says. I just knew it. The man pats you on the back and says: Remember me?

You look at him and you say, I don't know who the hell you are.

Of course, you *must* remember me! It was here I last saw you. You pulled the anchor from the wall and you handed it to me? You told me to carry it with me and never forget.

Forget what?

Forget this. The times we had together here when we were young. Do you remember now?

Vaguely, you say.

Let me buy you a beer he says, and so he does. Cheers. Prost. 'Ere's mud in your eye—to the good old days!

I've come to tell you I never forgot about you, no matter how our ways were parted, and though I thought I lost it, I recently discovered the anchor hook that you gave me. I found it in a box of stuff from my Chicago days. I've come to give it back to you and tell you that you were my dearest friend.

He hands you the anchor hook and he attempts to hug you. But you don't know what to say. So you say nothing. You raise your beer and you stare at him and you try to remember what it was you promised once so long ago to tell him.

Ten

FLAMINGO

And if you were to let go completely—how easy would that be? You try to think what the last sounds might be, and you go back to Herb Jeffries singing *Flamingo*. You can't describe why that is the last song you would want to hear—but on the other hand no one would understand if they hadn't lived your life precisely as you have lived it. There is the uplift of emotion that the song invariably provides—and there is the layered complicated emotional experience tied up in all the years you have wrapped up in the sound of that song playing endlessly on the jukebox while you sat at the bar drinking your beer. You have heard the song so many countless times it stands to reason that hearing it one final time—the moment before you let go—is the most appropriate end you can imagine for yourself. While you sit at the Bar having these thoughts, the bartender pours you a stein of beer and he offers this one 'on the house' in a rare gesture of gratitude. Does he know, or at least sense, that you're dying? That you loved your life—circumscribed though it was, sheltered though it was—in this dark and miserable hiding place?

Thank you, you say with absolute cordiality. You sip your beer. You listen to your song...*Flamingo, like a bird across the sky*...and you float out into the water just beyond where the pink flamingos stand on one leg in the pink and gorgeous light of day, and you tap your own foot slowly to the dying rhythm of the song.

Nine

FUCK'S SAKE

Who knows how many beers? Who the fuck is counting? You will be dead in three weeks, for fuck's sake! You are sitting there at the bar and the rage that this simple phrase conjures in you is more than you can handle. You step off your stool and you pick it up and you start swinging it over your head and you launch it across the room so it smashes against the wall and knocks a beer sign down and you nearly topple over yourself. Then you grab a chair at one of the Formica tables and you start smashing it against the table. This is what you mean to me, you say, swinging the chair down smashing it against the table. This is what all of you mean to me. You grab another chair and you start smashing it against the wall until the plaster breaks loose from the slats and the chair vibrates then splinters in your hands. There is the sound of a commotion behind you as they grab you and pull the chair from your hands and then they drop you to the floor, throw you on your belly, and grab your arm and yank it behind you, another grabbing your neck and head-locking you until. Until you are still and heaving for breath. Your eyesight is dead and smudged at the center and all you have left is the peripheral. You have bitten your tongue and blood is coming from your mouth and you are cussing the eyes of the mother who caused you such hurt and you will be dead. That's what you keep screaming at these fucks: I will be dead, for fuck's sake. Kill me now! Kill me! Don't you hear what

I'm saying! For fuck's sake kill me now, and spare me my other death.

Eight

BIRTHDAY

It's your birthday today, and this point is barely noticed by you. You thought to check the calendar earlier in the morning but you forgot to get around to it. Why did you forget to get around to it? Because there were moments during the day when the idea of your birthday slipped your mind altogether and you just went puttering about your day. Why keep the idea there? What's there to celebrate anymore? You are happy to sit alone at the bar in the mid-afternoon lull drinking your beer. For a while you sit there ignoring the sound of the TV, and you count beans. You take a spoonful of soup and count how many black beans are in each spoonful. The soup is hot, so you blow on the spoon of soup until it cools and you sip down, very carefully, your spoonful of three or four beans. You take a sip of beer then set your mug down on a coaster. You look outside the bar and see the flash of someone's head—balding, catching the summer light— as it bounces east along the window and is suddenly gone. Two more heads enter from the left side of the window and they bounce along until they exit window-right. Then there is a city bus that drives past and you close your eyes to see how long you can hear the droning noise that it makes until it is drowned out by other droning noises. Then you open your eyes and you gather another spoonful of soup. This time you count six beans in your spoon and you say to yourself, reflexively, I am a six. At that moment the idea of your birthday occurs to you and you also say, I am sixty-six. You blow on your soup as if it were a birthday candle, then you insert the spoon in your mouth. You reach for your mug of beer. The beer is nice and cold today. It cools your mouth down from the hot soup. You can already see the dew collecting on the glass. In a minute, you think, I'll have another beer.

Seven

THE STOOL

Today for reasons unknown to you—perhaps you are seeking change—you step into the Bar and instead of sitting in your customary stool, you notice the empty stool that Johnny Bright—known to everyone at the bar as Blind-eyed Bob—once occupied before he fell back off of his stool and died. You have spent the better part of the last six years staring across the bar at that spot, wondering about Johnny Bright. There are times you still expect him to walk into the place at his customary hour. When the clock ticks down to that moment you turn your head to the door and when Johnny Bright fails to appear you confirm once again that he is dead. Why hadn't I ever said a word to him? you wonder. We lived such different lives and yet our lives were not so different in the end. That's when, instead of sauntering to your stool, you saunter to his and take a seat. The bartender looks over at your stool and sees it empty and then looks to you sitting in Johnny Bright's stool. He lifts an eye in surprise, then the dulled bored look recovers itself on his face. He steps to you and asks: Will it be the same thing today or something new? You try to remember what Johnny Bright drank. Was it rum and Coke? You're not sure so you tell him: I'll have whatever Blind-eyed Bob had. Gin and tonic then? Yes, that suits me fine. He mixes the highball, he squeezes the lime and drops it into the drink, and he sets it on a coaster in front of you. You haven't had a gin and tonic in centuries, you think, and as you sip an infusion of joy grips your heart.

How nice to try something new—like Johnny Bright's favorite drink. I'll drink it in his honor! You lean back in the stool a bit to see if it's wobbly. I wonder if that's why he fell off this thing, you think, but no, it seems perfectly stable. A moment later you lean back so far you almost lose your balance. Your hands slap the bar as you try to catch yourself from falling. When you stabilize, you feel a slight lift of adrenaline touch the edge of your heart—as if you had been on a swing. You remember swinging as a boy in a park getting pushed in the pink light of morning by your grandfather as he stood in the shadows pushing you on the swing and drinking Meister Bräu from a bottle in a paper bag. You have spent so much of your time trying to purge yourself of memories of that man that you're suddenly surprised that this one is still in your mind. That's okay, you think. Purging it will give me something to do today. In the meantime, you look across the bar towards your stool. It's empty and its emptiness is staring back you. Goodbye, you say to yourself. Goodbye, whoever you were!

Six

HEATHER

Heather is standing there before you. She seems to have arrived suddenly and instantly from nowhere. She is standing directly and frankly in front of you and when you lift your gaze to look at her she returns it. She has a smile on her face—or rather she has a naturally smiling face, and this is one of the qualities that you have come to treasure in her. She looks at you and sees you for who you are, and unlike anyone else you have ever known, she is open to that. She does not judge. In other words, she understands precisely how you are calibrated; she knows your number, or combination of numbers. She gets your code and she finds it satisfactory. The fact that someone so lovely understands you seems to make that understanding lovely and somehow that loveliness touches you and makes you even a little bit lovely. It's a wild impossibility that you should have ever been or ever will be lovely—and yet with Heather standing there, hands on hips, looking at you—it comes within the realm of the possible. It's as if you had suddenly come up with a winning number on lottery day, or as if you were that winning number yourself. That's how you feel, anyways, during this improbable human moment brought on by Heather wherein she seems to implicitly confirm your tolerable loveliness.

Tell me Heather, you feel on the cusp of asking her: tell me something I have always wanted to know but have never been able to learn. Would you tell me please: precisely who and exactly what I am?

But instead you simply smile at her because that seems the most peaceful thing to do. And when she asks you on a whim what your favorite number is you tell her six. As in six pack. Unexpectedly she laughs, and so do you.

Five

THE LAST STATION

You have single-mindedly dedicated yourself to staying on this train to the end of the line. Whether you chose it or whether it chose you is a question that you no longer care to debate. You sit in your train car, the Bar, and watch time go by. There are times when you feel like you are slowly climbing a great mountain of time. You can almost hear the chug of the engine as it huffs and puffs its way through the days. You often wonder what will happen when you get on the other side of that mountain—what will the downward slope bring? Nothing good, you surmise—and you're probably right.

You passed your last waystation years ago without debarking. That was when your wife asked to meet you for lunch. It was a do-or-die meeting. Your marriage was on the ropes. Your daughter needed you. Your wife wanted you. You claimed to want them, but this was the luncheon where you would do more than make a claim: this was the luncheon where you would commit yourself to both your wife and your daughter. In the hours leading up to that luncheon, you thought there might be an opportunity to reconcile your differences with them. You thought that reconciliation with your wife and daughter might entail confessions of wrongdoing, promises that you would clean up your act—promises that you would fix what was broken, mend what had become frayed. But as your train was pulling through the moment, you decided to stay on and not get off, and in an hour all hope for reconciliation was behind you.

There are days even now you feel the powerful desire to jump off the train to retrace your steps back to that luncheon you set up with your wife. Though the problem now is: you are so far out on the empty steppe of your bender that you wouldn't know how to get back even if you wanted to. What might that station have been like if you had gotten off the train? You imagine a crush of people getting on and off—and a woman with pain and joy in her eyes searching the crowd for you who, with your own pain and joy, searches to meet her.

Four

THE STRANGER

You are enjoying your beer this afternoon and the songs coming over the jukebox are some of your favorite numbers. Nat King Cole is crooning in a lovely nostalgic voice a song about dancing and feeling on the cusp of something impossible and this song—his voice, the lyric—make you feel grand and limitless. Next on the jukebox is Billie Holiday singing *What A Little Moonlight Can Do*. The juxtaposition of the lightning-fast rhythm section with her slow-swinging voice never fails to make you happy and it's in this bubble of happiness when the door to the bar opens and in walks someone you've never seen before. She asks you if the barstool next to you is taken and when you tell her it isn't she sits down, dropping her bag on the floor with a *phlump*, and her heavy body following suit. She lifts her finger to get the bartender's attention, and when he appears she asks for a double scotch and soda with a lemon twist and a water back. When the bartender serves her she removes the sunglass from her eyes, pushing them up on her head, and she rummages through her bag for her change purse. She pulls out a couple of fives and sets them on the bar. The bartender turns to you and asks if you'd like a refresher to which you say, of course.

There the two of you sit for some time, sipping your drinks. Her eyes are turned up toward the TV and your eyes are staring into the bar-back mirror trying to get a better read on who this stranger is that has taken possession of the stool next to yours. There is something familiar about her, but you're not sure. When she finishes her drink, she asks for another. When the bartender asks, double? She says, but of course. She wears two large brass bangles on her wrist and she is rotating them on her wrist while the bartender serves her drink. When he asks you, you decide not and say, not.

The two of you continue to drink. She watches the TV while you continue to peak at her through the bar-back mirror. When she asks you if there is a Cubs game today, you say, I have no idea. The fact is: you might have had an idea, but you are so curious to know who this woman is that is seated down next to you that when she asks you the question the answer slips your mind. You intently focus your eyes on her, trying to figure out why she looks familiar. How do you know her? She looks like a person who looks intimately familiar but whom time has irrevocably changed. She looks like someone you once loved. She looks friendly enough even though time hasn't been friendly to her. Perhaps you'll ask her name, but then again, maybe not. Maybe it'd be better to just let bygones be bygones.

When she orders another double scotch with a lemon twist the bartender serves her then asks you if you'd like another. No, you say. I think I'll just settle up. You push some money his way and he rings you up. Elvis Presley is singing *Blue Moon of Kentucky* when you say farewell to the lady. Bye, she says—barely noticing you. That's when you step out of the Bar into the bewildering light of day where the cars on the street are whizzing by way too quickly.

Three

THE FINGER OF GOD

One day the finger of God appears out of nowhere and he touches you. Where does he touch you? Does he tap your shoulder? If so, which one? Your left shoulder or your right? Probably your right... But if he doesn't touch your shoulder then what does he touch? Does he touch the inner palm of your hand? Does he stroke your finger from the tip of your middle down to the v of the hand and then stroke the index on an upward swoop? Does he touch that space on your upper lip just beneath your nose, where the finger of God was thought to originally touch you? Or does he reach into you and pluck one of your lower rib bones, reminding you that from that single bone he could form a woman as precisely suited to you as Eve was to Adam? Does he tousle your hair like your baseball coach did once when you were a kid? You hit a triple and when you were RBI'd home and you trotted to the dugout your coach removed your batting helmet and tousled your hair like your father might have tousled your hair if he had ever shown some fatherly love. Would God, too, show some fatherly love? No, tonight, after drinking seventeen beers and two or three shots of brandy God touches you completely by a finger of wind. It's as if a holy wind blows through and around you, and the folding of you so completely into the hand of God brings the moment to a question. You're certain it's a question—what other thing would God utter to you? The question God asks is: Where have you been? You stare at the bar-back mirror and you mouth those words to yourself: Where have you been? Only it's not you mouthing the words—it's some external force—God himself—causing you to mouth these words. Why is it an external force? Because you would never ask yourself that question. Why would you? You know where you've been. You've been loyal to yourself every step of the whole godforsaken way.

Two

THE AGENDA

Today, your slate is clear. You have nothing on your calendar. You have no engagements, nor do you have anything of pressing urgency. It is a pause in your life, and when you come to the pause your instinct is to extend it as long as possible. The pause is all, you say to yourself, and what better way to extend it than by making a day of it at the Bar? You drift on over to the Bar earlier than usual, and you're waiting by the door when they open. The bartender asks you what you're doing here so early and you tell him: I have nothing to do today, nothing at all. I'm in the middle of a pause, so to speak, so I thought, why not come on down and see what you guys are doing?

Well come on in, the bartender says. We're awful glad to see you—even if it is first thing in the morning.

You find your spot. What a lovely spot it is this time of day! And the way the light fills the place, causing the chrome to gleam and the bar-back mirror to glimmer with spectral luminescence: it fills your heart with joy.

When the bartender asks what you'll have, the answer, though not obvious given who you are, suddenly seems perfectly reasonable. A Bloody Mary, you say. Why the hell not?

That sounds perfectly agreeable to me, the bartender says. A good way to get your vitamins! He reaches for the vodka, the tomato juice, the horseradish, the Tabasco sauce, the Worchester. He shakes it on ice in a shaker. He pours it into a pint glass with ice. He adds a shake of celery salt, and a garnish of olive, a celery-stick and a slice of lime and he serves it to you on a coaster. Cheers! he says and then he turns on the television and he puts the *Price is Right* on and soon, very soon, Drew Carey says, Come on Down! and with that your glorious day begins.

One

THE BOOK AND THE SONG

Whenever you hold a book in your hand you always jump to the last page and read it to see if it's worth reading all those previous pages just to get to here. You have been reading books all your life. In fact your favorite thing to do is to sit in the Bar, drink your beer and read. The books that you read continually tell you that you will die and when you die it shall be an unhappy death. You like reading these sorts of books because they confirm a truth that drinking in this bar all these years has confirmed: You are mortal. You will die. The way you die will be beyond your choosing, unless you kill yourself.

If you were a writer and this were your book—well then, you would like to blow up the word-bridge that connects the reader to your book. You are tired of watching the reader stare down the ladder of your words and into the well of your soul trying to gain access to the shadows and deeper shadows left by the tracings of your text; you are tired of those readerly eyes that feel their way all too intimately across the surface of your pages...like fingers across the skin, trying to decipher what is written there. The blind readerly hands touching your face, probing: is it wearing a smile? Is it wearing a frown? Is there anguish here? And if so, what is its cause?

You are tired of the mind behind those readerly eyes asking questions like these; tired of allowing that mind and those eyes to peer beneath the surface of the burnt-out runic symbiology you have left behind like ashen markings upon the page. That is why you want to blow up the word-bridge between yourself and the reader!

You want to say to the reader: All of this attention you have paid me, making your way to the final pages of my book, and for what? What are you looking for? Are you trying to find me, or are you trying to find yourself?

Let's end this battle for meaning that rages on...in other words, go to hell! *Kapooey! Blam!! Kapow!* In a moment the word-bridge is blown. But it will take a few moments to fall.

In the meantime you can go back to what you were doing, go back to incognito. You order a refill on your beer. You take a long sip off the foamy head of the beer and you stare into the bar-back mirror at those daffodils ringing your head like the mane of a lion. What a beautiful afternoon it is! And how nice to be drinking here unobserved. You look outside the window of the bar at the clouds and notice a V of geese—such wondrous wingèd things!—making their way in the upper blue and heading east toward the lake. A ribbon of song enters your mind...or is it coming from the jukebox? Hard to say, because mind and jukebox have become one. You are the Guy Lombardo singing to the You that is you.

> *Enjoy yourself it's later than you think*

> *Enjoy yourself while you're still in the pink...*

It's such a lovely melody; you want to cry from the beauty...

Let life do with you what it pleases. You are quite sure it pleases nothing nice. Why should it? You're a mortal, after all. But it is by being so enamored by the soft pink light of late afternoon that you have found a way to escape unnoticed and outside the ken of time. At such moments notions of mortality and how yours shall be affected fade from view and what moves into view are the lovely tangibles: the long-varnished top of this old and dented bar scuffed by glass and elbow and the light shimmering off its surface. You hear a droning sound. Is it a wasp trapped in the tin-can of your molar? Or is it the noise of a bee buzzing in the flower cup of one of those glowing daffodils? Why not have another sip of beer and enjoy yourself! Enjoy yourself, while you're still in the pink.

But occasionally, another melody finds its way to the surface of your consciousness, and there it swims green and fish-like, a useless strand of thought plying the waters of the mind until, after a handful of beers, you drown it. For a while, though, you will let it have its way. Why not? It is a repetitious song, but it ends, and you don't know what you like better, the fact that it is repetitious, or the fact that it ends. But you can sing it. Why not? Or hum it, at least. You have nothing else to do this afternoon but hum ditties and drink beer... hum...drink beer... hum...drink beer... hum...drink beer...hum....drink beer...hum....

> *Ninety-nine bottles of beer on the wall, ninety-nine bottles of beer...*

> *Take one down, pass it around, ninety-eight bottles of beer on the wall...*

Ninety-eight bottles of beer on the wall, ninety-eight bottles of beer...

Take one down, pass it around, ninety-seven bottles of beer on the wall...

Ninety-seven bottles of beer on the wall, ninety-seven bottles of beer...

Take one down, pass it around, ninety-six bottles of beer on the wall...

ABOUT THE AUTHOR

Joseph G. Peterson is the author of several books of fiction and poetry, including, most recently, *Gunmetal Blue*. He grew up in Wheeling, Illinois, attended the University of Chicago, and he worked for several years at Jimmy's Woodlawn Tap. He currently lives in Chicago, where he works in publishing.

"One of my new favorite authors [is] Joseph G. Peterson."
- Rick Kogan, WGN Radio

ABOUT TORTOISE BOOKS

Slow and steady wins in the end, even in the publishing industry. Tortoise Books is dedicated to finding and promoting quality authors who haven't yet found a niche in the marketplace—writers producing memorable and engaging works that will stand the test of time.

Learn more at www.tortoisebooks.com, find us on Facebook, or follow us on Twitter @TortoiseBooks.

CPSIA information can be obtained
at www.ICGtesting.com
Printed in the USA
LVHW110512020719
622836LV00002BA/275/P